A boy called
OCEAN

CHRIS
HIGGINS

Hodder
Children's
Books

HODDER CHILDREN'S BOOKS

First published in Great Britain in 2018 by Hodder and Stoughton

1 3 5 7 9 10 8 6 4 2

A CIP catalogue record for this book
is available from the British Library.

ISBN 978 0 340 99703 1

Typeset in Berkeley Oldstyle by Hewer Text UK Ltd, Edinburgh
Printed and bound in Great Britain by Clays Ltd, St Ives plc

Hodder Children's Books
An imprint of Hachette Children's Group
Part of Hodder and Stoughton
Carmelite House
50 Victoria Embankment
London EC4Y 0DZ

An Hachette UK Company
www.hachette.co.uk

A boy called
OCEAN

For Twig and our lovely family.
Thank you for being with me every step of the way.

PROLOGUE

The sun is already starting to dip beneath the horizon as I reach the beach. It's high tide. I'm cutting it fine.

Second thoughts? No way. After everything that's happened, I need this.

Before I can change my mind I wrap the leash round my ankle and charge into the sea, holding the board in front of me like a shield. Splashing my way through the white water, I take a deep breath and hurl myself into the ocean.

Resurfacing, I gasp in shock as the cold hits me. I shake the water from my hair and start paddling my way out across a golden pathway of light towards the red ball of the sun. As I duck-dive under the waves all the bad stuff starts to recede. By the time I've made it out back and am sitting up, my mind is clear. *Magic.*

I wait for the first decent wave, see one worth paddling for, then realise I'm too late and let it go. There will be more. Suddenly I have all the time in the world.

Before long my patience is rewarded and I spot a set of waves coming. As it gets closer I let the first one go, and the second, then get ready for the third. This is it. A good one.

I stand up and start to move across the wave, feeling its strength beneath me. I try out some turns and to my delight they work until, over-excited, I twist too fast and tumble in head first. No matter. I paddle out for more. This is it – the best feeling in the world!

My next wave is a mistake. It's too steep. I take off but nosedive, banging my head on the sand. I'm held under by the power of the wave and taste sudden, sharp fear. It feels like someone's standing on my back, pinning me down; it can only be seconds but feels like a lifetime.

As soon as I swim back to the surface all fear is gone. Grabbing my board I head out again, hoping the next one will be better.

I sit back and wait. My head's killing me but it's worth it. I am alone with the ocean. I am free.

Another wave comes. A really good one. I catch it this time and, "Whoa!" For the first time in my life I'm carving it! Twisting and turning, I keep going, edging my way to the back of the board. I'm doing it, I'm in control! Until finally, inevitably, the wave opens up and pushes me out.

I pull away, exhilarated, triumphant, drained, and sink slowly into the sea.

That was it. The perfect wave.

The sun has gone leaving a brilliant red line but I can still see clearly. The waves call to me and I can't resist them.

Just one more . . .

I paddle back out and sit waiting patiently. Time ceases to exist. I feel calm, at peace with the world, all tension and conflict gone. Before my eyes the incredible red, pink and orange-streaked sky melts into the horizon, blending with the oily blue-black sea to form a glorious explosion of colour like a huge abstract painting. I am lost in the wonder of it all.

Suddenly I want to share this moment with the person closest to me in the world, but I can't. A sense of loss pierces me, as sharp as a knife wound.

The ocean is flat now. There are no more waves.

I shiver. I'm beginning to get cold and tired.

Time to head in.

As I turn round to face the shore I realise to my surprise how far I have drifted out. An offshore breeze has whipped itself up and Porthzellan Cove is almost invisible beneath a bank of solid grey cloud. I strike out for shore, paddling strongly against the wind. It shouldn't take me long.

After a while I stop paddling and lift my head to check where I am. *What?* I am stunned to see that I am even further out now, almost to the headland. *How did that happen?* I sit upright on my board, confused. True, the wind has picked up, but I've managed worse. And then I understand.

The tide has turned. *How stupid am I?* It's taking me out. In the short time I've been sat up I've moved beyond the headland.

Quickly I lie back down on the board and start to power my arms furiously through the water. I call on all my reserves of strength, every muscle in my body fired by my determination to get back to safety. *I'm stronger than I look, I can do this.*

But when at last I pause for breath, I can feel the wind has intensified and the sea has got rougher. And even before I lift my head to peer through the darkness, I can tell that I have left the rocky shelter of Porthzellan Cove far behind and am adrift in the open sea.

Too late I realise something else.

Nobody knows where I am.

PART
ONE

PART
ONE

chapter 1
KAI

Kai had been trying to get hold of Jen all morning. He'd been late for school – as usual! Then he'd missed her at break time because she was on library duty, and Kai was banned from the library (unfairly in his opinion – it wasn't inappropriate use of a computer, it was research). He'd looked for her throughout lunchtime until someone said she was probably in the hall, rehearsing for the autumn show.

That was Jen. Busy, popular, successful, involved in absolutely everything. And yet, to his eternal surprise, it was him she wanted to be with.

He peered through the glass panel of the door hoping to get her attention but she was nowhere to be seen. His stomach sank. *Where was she?* He needed to speak to her.

Then he spotted her in the far corner of the hall demonstrating a dance routine and grinned in relief. She never changed. In charge, as usual.

They went back a long way, he and Jen, to primary school in fact. He cringed as he remembered how he'd arrived in the far west of Cornwall around the age of four with a hippy mum, the wrong accent and long hair like a girl's.

He'd been practically feral in those days, running round semi-naked all day long like Mowgli. Only his jungle was Porthzellan Cove and his mum was definitely no wolf. *More like prey*, he thought.

But it was OK. As soon as he started school, Jen had taken him under her wing. She'd shouted at the boys who'd laughed at him, tugged his hair back into a ponytail so tightly he'd thought his scalp was coming off, and said she liked him best.

They'd been best friends ever since and before long he'd been totally accepted into Sandy Bay. He had Jen to thank for that. She led and he followed, that was the way it worked. They were inseparable.

Over the years little had changed. Until this summer, that is, the year they were both fifteen. Things had shifted. Maybe it was because he'd shot up, filled out a bit, too. For the first time in his life he was taller than Jen, and still growing. Now she was the one looking up to him!

She was different, too. In a good way. Loads more tactile than she used to be, Jen had started acting like they were a proper couple. She was always hanging on to his arm, stroking his back when they were talking to others, hugging him, kissing him hello and goodbye.

It was weird.

It was wonderful.

It was confusing.

Jen was gorgeous. He wanted to kiss her too; proper kisses that lasted for more than one second. But how could he? She was his best mate.

And what if he'd got it wrong? The last thing he wanted to do was ruin their friendship.

The bell went for afternoon school and Kai groaned. He daren't be late again or he'd get a detention. And then he'd be late for work and *then* all his carefully laid plans for tonight would go wrong. Tentatively he opened the door.

'Out!' bawled Miss Todd.

'Six o'clock, Beach Café! Don't be late!' he shouted. Jen turned, grinned and stuck her thumb up and everyone laughed except for the drama teacher. Kai let out a sigh of relief and scarpered before she could get hold of him.

Jen had got the message. She'd be there.

He'd been gearing himself up to this for ages. Now the time had come for him to take the initiative for once in his life. After school he was working an hour or two as usual at the Beach Café, clearing tables. But tonight, unbeknown to Jen, when the families had left and the couples came out to dine, he had booked a table for two.

The best table, on the balcony. The one overlooking the Pass.

It was time to make their relationship official.

And tonight he was going to do it properly.

chapter 2

JEN

'Beach at six?' said Ellie when Miss Todd had finally let them go. 'Mind if I tag along too?'

'To see Kai?' teased Jen.

Ellie frowned. 'No! To see Macca, of course.'

Oops! *Said the wrong thing there*, thought Jen. To her great surprise, Ellie had had a bit of a thing about Kai earlier in the year, but it had come to nothing. It was obvious to everyone, even Ellie eventually, that he wasn't interested. In fact, he was totally oblivious to her.

Jen thought she'd got over it by now but apparently she was still touchy.

'Macca's awesome!' added Ellie.

'Macca's *awesome*!' parroted Jen. 'You even sound like him! What are you like?'

'Everyone fancies Macca!' Ellie protested.

'*I* don't!'

'Only because you're all loved-up with Kai,' said Ellie, sourly.

Jen rolled her eyes. Sometimes she felt years older than her friend. Macca had been THE summer sensation at Sandy Bay. Tall, bronzed and Australian, Martin Mackenzie, the new beach lifeguard with his long, sun-streaked hair and easy, laid-back manner, had been an instant hit with everyone when he'd arrived at the start of the season. Especially the girls.

Ellie had a point though. Macca was seriously fit, there was no doubt about it.

'No, it's just that Macca doesn't do it for me. Like, he's a really nice guy but there's no . . . mystery . . . to him, if you know what I mean.'

'Yeah! Unlike Kai! That's my point. You compare everyone with him.'

Jen shook her head at her friend's persistence but recognised the truth of what she was saying. Slim and slight, with thick dark hair, the ponytail having disappeared years ago, thank goodness, though his fringe still fell into his deep brown eyes, there was so much more to Kai than most people realised.

Jen knew him better than anyone else in the world and yet sometimes she wasn't sure she knew him at all. He was always surprising her with the things he said, the things he did. Most people didn't get him. They liked him enough, but he was a bit of a loner. He could come across as quiet, awkward, moody, a bit of a wimp almost, compared with the macho rugby boys and the regular surfing crowd.

But he wasn't, not at all. He was deep and complex and different from anyone else she knew, and that's what appealed to her.

Kai was so many things. He was a complete paradox. She couldn't help smiling at the thought of him.

Kai was thoughtful and a dreamer. He could also be impetuous and disorganised, his home life, over the years, being a tad chaotic. He read more than anyone else she knew, wrote poems, loved Shakespeare, was into music, not just pop and grime but other earlier stuff she didn't get at all. At the same time he was equally at one with the elements and the natural world, and was far, far tougher than he looked. Mr Davis who took them for English really rated him. Most of the other teachers thought he was trouble, probably because of his habit of bolting out of class when things went wrong.

All this, combined with his cute smile, the way his eyes lit up when he saw her and the fact he was way taller than her now, she found incredibly sexy.

This had come as a big shock to Jen. She hadn't expected to feel like this about Kai. She didn't know how to deal with it and it was driving her mad.

'I can tell you're thinking about him, you've got that look on your face. Admit it, Jen! You're besotted with him,' said Ellie.

Jen groaned inwardly. She blamed Ellie. It was her fault. Hers and one or two other girls at school who had recently woken up to the fact that strange little Kai had grown up and morphed into someone intriguing and pretty fit.

It was like they'd alerted her to the possibility of a romance with her best friend. Weird! Weird! Weird! But she couldn't stop thinking about it.

The worst thing was, she had no idea if Kai felt the same.

After school they went back to Ellie's. The two girls had been friends since their very first show together at Sandy Bay High. Ellie, small and lively, was terrified of missing out and always up for everything. She blitzed through life like a mini tornado, following every single trend, whereas Jen, taller and more alternative, wasn't afraid to do her own thing and be different. Despite that they were good mates – most of the time.

Jen flopped onto Ellie's bed and checked her phone to see if there was a message from Kai. Nothing. He'd be at work by now at the Beach Café. She wondered what all the fuss was about, telling her to be there on time, bang on six o'clock. She smiled to herself. That was rich, coming from him.

She couldn't wait to see him later.

'What shall I wear?'

Ellie was busy tearing clothes from her wardrobe, holding them up for inspection then flinging them down on her bed. Jen picked up a sparkly dress from the growing pile with raised eyebrows.

'Uh? Can I remind you that we're going to the beach?'

'I don't like it anyway,' said Ellie, snatching it back. 'What about these?' She held up a pair of jeans with rips in the knees.

'Better. But they're your dancing ones.'

'So? Who says I won't end up dancing with someone by the end of the night?' She whirled round and round the room with a daft, dreamy look on her face, clutching the jeans to her. Jen laughed out loud.

'Who might that be, then? As if I didn't know.'

'Oh no!' Ellie came to an abrupt standstill. 'I've got less time than I thought to drive Macca wild. I just remembered, I promised Mum I'd babysit later. Right, I've got to up my game. Yes? No?' She waved a pair of miniscule shorts at Jen.

'Bit unsubtle.'

'That's me, babe!' She shook her head in mock exasperation at her friend and pulled them on regardless. 'D'you know what, Jen? Sometimes you remind me of my mum! What are you wearing anyway?'

Jen glanced at her watch. 'I was going home to change but it's getting a bit late.'

'D'you want to borrow something?'

'It's okay, we'll probably just be sitting around on the beach.'

Ellie stared at her. 'You cannot hang out at Sandy Bay in your school uniform!'

'Why not?' Jen glanced out at the blue sky. 'Okay, maybe I'll change into my shorts and trainers.'

'Tell me you're joking!' Ellie watched in horror as Jen fished inside her bag for her PE kit. 'Look, put this on at least.' She threw an off -the -shoulder top at her friend.

'But it's brand new. You only bought it on Saturday. You haven't even worn it yet.'

'So?' Ellie, generous to a fault, was more concerned about replacing her school studs with big hoops. "I'm not going to the beach with you looking like a div!'

Jen gasped. 'Are you allowed to say that?' Then, 'What is a div, anyway?'

'I dunno.'

The two girls laughed and finished dressing, continuing to swap jokes and friendly insults. When they were ready they stared at themselves in the full-length mirror.

'That top looks loads better on you than it does on me,' said Ellie, sounding a bit wistful. 'I wish I was tall like you. Look how long your legs are! It's not fair. You look great, even in your PE shorts.'

'So do you,' said Jen and gave her a hug. And Ellie really did look nice in her skimpy shorts, flimsy top and hoop earrings. Though personally, she wouldn't have been seen dead in them.

'Wait a sec.' Ellie tugged on a pair of lace-up heeled sandals, stretched herself up to her full height and examined herself in the mirror with satisfaction. 'That's better. Look, I'm nearly as tall as you now. Perhaps Macca will notice me at last.'

Jen shook her head in despair at her fickle friend. Rejected by Kai, Ellie had found it easy to transfer her affections to Macca and now she was obsessing about him non-stop even though last year it had been all about the other lifeguards on Sandy Bay, Ben and Danny, and Jen's cousin, Jay.

How could two mates be so different? She'd never wanted to be with anyone but Kai.

'Come on,' sighed Jen. 'We're going to be late.'

She should have let it go. But as they ran down the lane towards Sandy Bay together, she continued, 'Anyway, El, admit it. You only fancy Macca because he's a lifeguard.'

She was rewarded with howls of protest.

'No way! It's his accent I love.'

'What? Everything he says sounds like a question.'

'And the way he smiles. His eyes crinkle up.'

'That's because he's had too much sun,' said Jen, unkindly.

'Shut up! His eyes are gorgeous. *He's* gorgeous. He's so friendly. I feel like I've known him for ages.'

Jen did her famous eyebrow-raising face. 'You've known him about five months.'

'So? That's long enough,' declared Ellie, beginning to sound nettled. 'Just because you and Kai have been together for ever.'

'Me and Kai? I'm not going out with Kai.'

'Yeah, right! "Meet me after work, Jen. See you at the Beach at six, Jen."'

Where did that come from? Jen stared at her friend in surprise. Ellie's silly high voice was infuriating. Kai didn't sound a bit like that.

16

'Don't deny it, Jen,' said Ellie. 'You two are together.'

'Not in that way! We're mates, that's all.'

'Come on, admit it!' shrieked Ellie. 'You've gone bright red!'

'No I haven't!' Jen could feel her cheeks on fire. She wanted to slap Ellie. Hard. Or rather, she wanted to tell her, *Yes, you're right, we are together, so there!*

But how could she? Because they weren't. Not yet, anyway. And if Kai didn't feel the same way as her, they never would be, no matter how much she wanted it. She knew that for certain after what had happened between him and Ellie.

Maybe he just wanted to be friends.

Aargh! This was so frustrating. And still Ellie wouldn't shut up. 'Jen, admit it! You've always had a thing for him.'

'Don't be daft.' Ellie was really getting on her nerves.

'Kai snaps his fingers and you come running. It's always been the same. You're a soft touch where he's concerned.'

'That is so not true!' Jen glared at Ellie. How dare she?

She had a mind of her own. She didn't run after anyone. Did she?

chapter 3
MACCA

Martin Mackenzie from New South Wales, Australia, had little idea of the effect he was having on the female teen population of Sandy Bay, Cornwall.

As a lifeguard, Macca, as he was known to one and all, was used to being asked questions about tides and rip currents but, until his new colleagues informed him otherwise, he had assumed these questions sprang from a genuine need to know the answer. Therefore, having fairly recently swotted up on local knowledge, he readily passed it on with enthusiasm to grateful enquirers who, now he came to think about it, were often young girls, like the trio who had just arrived on the beach after school.

After he'd answered all their questions and directed them to a safe area to enter the water, he came back to find the other lifeguards chuckling away amongst themselves.

'What's so funny?'

Jay looked at him pityingly.

'They don't want to go surfing, dipstick!'

Macca was confused. 'They said they did.'

'Duh! So where are their boards?'

Macca shrugged. 'I guess they're going to hire them at the shop.'

'You're hilarious, mate,' Danny chipped in. 'You still don't get it. They're just trying to get off with you, birdbrain!'

'It's your Aussie charm that turns them on.'

'It's the twang that does it.'

'And his curls.' They all burst out laughing.

Macca scratched his head and laughed, enjoying the banter. Tall, with sun-bleached hair that hung down over his ears in thick, salty twists, a deep tan left over from the Cornish summer and the Australian sun that preceded it and a six-pack honed from years of surfing, Macca didn't give a stuff about his looks and had very little interest in the girls who were so impressed by them.

He lived for one thing and one thing only: surfing.

Which was what had brought him to Sandy Bay in the first place. He wanted to surf the Pass. He'd met Jay while surfing six months ago at Byron Bay in Australia at a place also called the Pass. And when Jay told him that where he came from in the UK there was a place with the same name and a brilliant set of waves, Macca decided, on the spur of the moment, to make it summer all year round and come back with Jay to Cornwall to try it out. It was as good a reason as any.

Macca travelled light. He'd arrived in Sandy Bay with nothing but his passport and a board he'd bought on eBay, a retro single fin Bruce Palmer, 7-foot collectible. He and Jay had picked it up in Devon on the way down. He'd always hankered after one and it didn't disappoint, being slower, cruisier, thicker and more stable than any other board he'd ever owned. He didn't need anything else.

He'd bedded down at Jay's and before long had joined him and the others as a lifeguard on Sandy Bay where he was proving a hit, not just with the girls but with the rest of the team, because of his expertise and abundant enthusiasm.

Not that they ever told him that, of course.

'Uh-oh, here come some more fans.' Ben had spotted some girls wending their way along the beach. 'Isn't that your cousin and her mate, Jay?'

Jay narrowed his eyes and saw Jen and her friend coming towards them. 'Yep. Watch out, Mac.'

'I thought she went around with that hippy kid who helps out at the café,' said Danny. 'What's his name?'

'Kai. She does. But Ellie, the other one, is a Macca fan, you can tell.'

Ben groaned. 'We need a name for them. What shall we call them?'

'Macca Pakkas,' said Danny, who fancied himself as a bit of a wit, and everyone roared.

Macca shook his head with a grin. *What were they on about now?* Sometimes he felt he didn't speak the same language as these guys.

'Kids' programme on TV,' explained Jay, taking pity on him.

'Ah! The one you watch every night before you go to bed,' said Macca, joining in the joke, even though he had no idea what they were talking about.

'Sends me to sleep,' agreed Jay, which led to another round of laughter.

'What's so funny?' asked Jen as she came into earshot.

'I've just been telling the guys I watch *In the Night Garden* every night.'

'Better get home or you'll miss it then,' said Jen, laughing. 'You guys are weird.'

'Oops! Swimmers in the surfing area,' said Ben and grabbed the megaphone. 'Danny, move those flags up the beach a bit. It's nearly high tide.'

The two of them sprinted towards the shoreline and Jen gave her cousin a hug. She was dead proud of him. Recently he'd been taken on as the newest crew member of the Sandy Bay lifeboat.

Then she gave Macca one too so he wouldn't feel left out.

She was rewarded by the look of envy on Ellie's face, when he hugged her back with typical Aussie warmth, lifting her right off her feet.

chapter 4

KAI

Kai examined the table he had personally got ready for the umpteenth time.

Then he smoothed the already smooth tablecloth, straightened the perfectly aligned cutlery, polished the shiny glasses and moved the candle a millimetre to the right.

Then he rearranged the flowers he'd nicked from the garden of a holiday home on his way to work.

Then he placed the reserved sign on it.

He'd reserved a wine cooler too, hoping that Oliver, his employer and the head chef of the café, might have forgotten how old he was and chuck in a complimentary bottle of bubbly. After all, he'd let him reserve the very best table on the balcony, and promised to make them his pre-dinner, world-famous, Sandy Bay cocktails, on the house.

It had been his mum's idea. 'Why don't you take Jen for a meal at that nice restaurant now you're earning a bit,' she'd said. She liked Jen and knew more than anyone how important she was to him.

She didn't know what he had planned though.

Kai sighed with pleasure. Jen had been angling for an invite ever since he'd started working at the Beach Café. She was going to love it, being wined and dined here, without any of their mates getting in the way. He hoped it would put her in the mood for his big reveal.

He'd thought about it a lot. Let's face it, he thought about everything a lot but this dinner was really important. It wasn't like he was going to ask her to marry him or anything, though he felt as nervous as if he was. He'd planned it down to the last detail.

He checked the clock again. The evening workers knew something was up, he could tell by the way Maggie, the washer-upper, and Dee, one of the waitresses, kept glancing over at him all dewy-eyed and giggling.

He ignored them and took a deep breath. What he intended to do was move things onto a new level. He'd seen the ways other boys looked at Jen recently.

He'd never been the one to take the first step. He'd always followed Jen's lead, right from the first moment they'd met. But now it was time to take the initiative. Because, for once in his life he knew exactly what he wanted.

He wanted them to be officially boyfriend and girlfriend. Then there would be no need to worry about some random jerk pinching her from under his nose and whisking her away.

And . . . he would finally get to kiss her properly.

Mum said that in the olden days, when she was a teenager, they used to call it going steady. It must have been loads easier in Mum's day. More straightforward.

Though it hadn't been straightforward for her, had it?

Anyway, enough of that. Tonight was the night. He'd made his mind up. Over dinner, he was going to tell Jen how he felt, ask her out, and see if she felt the same.

BIG IF!

Kai could feel his nerves getting the better of him and he pushed them down firmly. Of course she felt the same. All those hugs and little kisses she'd been giving him? What was all that about if it didn't mean she fancied him?

She should be here any minute. Unlike him, she was always punctual. Maybe it was something to do with wearing a watch.

He glanced over the balcony and grinned. Unbelievable. There she was, reliable as ever, walking up the beach with her mate Ellie, and looking gorgeous as usual. While Ellie was stumbling along the sand wearing high heels, barefoot Jen, carrying her trainers, had a natural grace and long-legged ease that turned heads.

The lifeguards had noticed her. They couldn't take their eyes off her. His stomach clinched.

He watched as she approached them and joined in some general laughter. She gets on with everyone, he thought.

He watched as two of the lifeguards ran off down the beach. Jen leant across and gave one of those remaining a hug.

Kai's eyes narrowed then his face cleared. It was OK. It was Jay, her cousin.

He watched as she turned to the other one and gave him a hug too and he hugged her back, lifting her clean off her feet.

Kai scowled as her arms tightened around him and she laughed out loud. *It's that new guy*, he thought. *The Aussie, Macca*. The one all the girls rave about. He felt his stomach drop.

Jen, still with her arm round his neck, caught sight of Kai and waved. 'Come on down.' she yelled.

He took a deep breath, feeling like he was coming out of a trance. 'On my way.' he shouted and headed for the stairs.

Down in the restaurant he was surprised to find people milling around. Oliver and Dee were looking frazzled.

'Kai, there you are!' shouted Oliver in relief. 'I need you to work on for a bit, mate. Laura's just called in to say she and Dave are going to be late. Their car's broken down.'

'But . . ." said Kai. He flung his arms out. 'I'm supposed to be . . .'

'No buts. I wouldn't ask but I've got this big party in. It's not for long.' Oliver dumped a pile of menus into Kai's hands and said abruptly, 'Just get this lot sat down and give these out for me. Quick as you can.'

chapter 5

JEN

Jen left Ellie flirting with Macca and strolled over to the Beach Café to meet Kai but there was no sign of him. She peered through the glass door and saw to her surprise that it was busy inside. There he was, showing people to their seats. She'd wait outside for him so as not to get in the way.

Ten minutes later, people were still pouring in and Kai was *still* getting them settled and totally unaware of her waiting. This was not on.

Why had Kai told her to meet him at six if he was going to carry on working? It looked like he'd forgotten all about her. She tried to attract his attention through the glass door but he was completely focused on what he was doing. Now he was doling out menus.

She had been so looking forward to spending the evening with him. Now she was annoyed with herself for building it up into something more significant than it actually was.

'Don't be late,' Kai had said. The cheek of it! She was never late, unlike him. For once in his life couldn't he make an arrangement and keep to it?

She wasn't going to spend her Friday night sitting on the steps of the Beach Café for anyone. Aggrieved, Jen reluctantly decided to make her way back to the others.

Way before she got there she could hear Ellie's raucous laughter. Macca was entertaining everyone with a stream of corny surfing jokes.

Ellie's obvious over-reaction to them added to Jen's worsening mood. She was way too loud and fake.

'They're not even funny,' she muttered to Jay. 'Just sexist and derogatory.'

Jay gave her a nudge. 'Lighten up, Jen! Where's your sense of humour?'

'Why is a surfboard better than a girlfriend?' continued Macca. 'Because a surfboard doesn't mind how many other surfboards you have.'

Ellie's screeches reached a new decibel high. Jen groaned and flung herself down on the sand, pressing her hands to her ears.

Ellie looked at her sourly. 'What's up with you? Your boyfriend late again? Timekeeping's not exactly his thing is it? Though I thought you'd be used to that by now.'

With an effort Jen ignored her, but Ellie persisted. 'I could have sworn I heard him say he was on his way.'

'He is,' said Jen shortly. 'They're busy, that's all. And he's not *my boyfriend*.'

'Girls, girls, girls,' said Macca, trying to defuse the situation.

Patronising idiot! As Ellie tittered like he'd said something amusing, Jen felt her fists clenching. She was so annoying! Jen was struggling to remind herself why exactly they were friends in the first place.

'Time to wind up here,' said Ben and the lifeguards started packing up. Ellie looked crestfallen.

Jay grabbed his stuff. 'Anyone fancy heading over to the Pass?'

Macca's eyes lit up. 'Sure. I might nip home and get Bruce first.'

'Who's Bruce?' asked Ellie. 'Is he a mate of yours?'

Jen rolled her eyes and Jay burst out laughing.

'My best mate,' answered Macca. 'He's my surfboard. A Bruce Palmer special.'

Ellie nodded knowledgeably.

Like she'd know what that meant, thought Jen grimly. Ellie hung around surfers but avoided the water like the plague. She might get her hair wet.

'I'll walk back with you if you want. I could do with the exercise,' offered Ellie eagerly.

'No time,' said Jay. 'The tide'll be on the turn before long and the weather's changing too.' He was always well up on sea conditions, even more so now he was on the lifeboat. 'If you want to catch some waves Mac, use your rescue board. We need to go now. Coming, Jen?'

Jen, he knew of old, was a pretty confident surfer who could handle the Pass.

'No thanks. I haven't got my stuff with me.'

'We could go and watch,' said Ellie even though the invitation hadn't strictly included her.

Jen hesitated. 'I'm waiting for Kai.'

'As usual. Though he doesn't seem to be around, does he?"

The two girls glared at each other. You could cut the tension with a knife.

'Go and see if he's ready," said Jay. 'We'll hang on for you.'

'No need. You guys head off without me,' said Jen and turned and ran across to the café. Kai had to be ready by now. When she got there she looked back and noticed that Jay, Macca and, of course, Ellie, who was clearly never going to let Macca out of her sight, were still waiting for her.

Jen sighed heavily, pushed open the door and walked inside.

chapter 6
KAI

Kai had never worked so hard in his life.

He and Dee had managed to get the big party settled, which was easier said than done as latecomers kept on pouring through the doors and upsetting the seating arrangements.

For the first time in his life he got why teachers complained when kids were late to a class. It was like, *really* disruptive. Everyone wanted to stop and talk or sit by their mates, and people kept getting up and swapping seats. Now he knew how Mr Davis felt as he tried to manage their unruly form. Only this lot were twice as old and twice as hard to organise.

When they were finally seated to their satisfaction he handed out the rest of the menus at top speed and, taking his cue from Dee, took their drinks orders as well. Then he decided it was time to make his bid for freedom. But just as he was slipping out of the door, Oliver came through from the kitchen looking flustered.

'Where are you going?' demanded Oliver.

'Home. I mean . . .'

He was about to amend that to 'meeting Jen' but stopped when he saw Oliver shaking his head. Kai stared blankly at him.

'I've done it. Everything. They're all sitting down and I've given out the menus like you asked me to. I've even taken their drinks orders.'

Oliver ran his hands through his thick, wavy hair, a sure sign he was getting stressed. 'Thanks Kai. Well done. But I need you to stay on, mate. Dave's rung in again. They're miles away and still waiting for the RAC. You and Maggie will have to cover for them tonight.'

'But . . .'

'Sorry!' Oliver held both hands up in front of him. 'No arguments, Kai. I haven't got time for this. You're one of the team and this is an emergency.'

Kai stared at him, dismayed. He'd obviously forgotten all about his big date with Jen and the table waiting for them on the balcony.

This was all going wrong.

He could refuse, he knew he could. But then he'd be letting Oliver down and he didn't want to do that. He liked his job even if it was just clearing tables. It meant he could plan special treats like dinner tonight for Jen and didn't have to rely on his mum for handouts. He could buy a decent phone. He could save up for a board like Macca's.

31

Kai wasn't daft. He knew he had a reputation at school for being flaky: for never being on time; for running away when things got too much to handle. It was too late to do much about that. But to his surprise he'd got on OK at the café. He'd never been late, not once, and was quietly learning loads about running a successful business. He'd even found himself hoping that one day maybe he could be a chef like Oliver and own his own restaurant.

You're one of the team, Oliver had said. This could be his chance to show his boss what he was made of.

Anyway, he could hardly sit upstairs wining and dining Jen while they were all struggling down here.

'Take the orders and get them through to me pronto,' instructed Oliver. 'The sooner we get this show on the road, the sooner you can go home.'

Kai nodded. It would be OK, he told himself. Knowing her, Jen would come looking for him soon and then he could ask her to wait for him. It was no big deal, she wouldn't mind. After all, it wasn't like she had any idea about his carefully laid plans.

When the rush was over he'd remind Oliver of his date and then he'd be really sorry and cook them a special dinner to make amends. It would just be a bit later than planned, that's all. And Jen would be proud of him for stepping up to the mark. It was exactly the sort of thing she would do in the same situation.

Oliver disappeared into the kitchen.

Kai picked up a pad and got on with it.

chapter 1

JEN

Jen stared in surprise around the crowded Beach Café. Normally one of the most exclusive venues around to dine in the evening, the sort of place she dreamt of coming to, tonight it was packed to the hilt with a large noisy crowd.

There was no sign of Kai. A guy twice her age and already the worse for wear lurched towards her and she stepped back. Behind her somebody squawked and she turned around to apologise.

It was Ellie.

'Wow!' she breathed, her eyes wide. 'It's crazy in here.'

'Why are you following me?' asked Jen, furiously.

'To tell you to get a move on,' said Ellie. 'The guys won't budge without you. Give me a break Jen, this is my big chance with Macca. Where's Kai by the way?'

'There he is.' Jen spotted him coming out of the kitchen and made a beeline for him with Ellie in tow.

'What are you doing?'

'Waiting.' He grinned and held two plates in his hands up high to show her.

He looked so pleased with himself Jen had to smile. But then Ellie stuck her nose in.

'No, it's us who are waiting, Kai. For you, as usual.'

Kai looked alarmed. 'What's it got to do with you? It's Jen I'm meeting tonight, not you.'

'Charming!' Ellie looked even more put out.

Jen tried to ignore her. 'So why did you ask me to meet you at six if you're still working at seven?' she asked, trying to be reasonable.

'I didn't know. Oliver asked me to work on. It's not my fault . . .' He moved past them and put the plates down in front of two customers.

'It never is,' muttered Ellie. 'He could've said no.'

'Butt out!' snapped Jen.

Kai turned back to them and frowned, catching their mood. 'I saw you. Earlier on. With Macca.'

'So?' Jen frowned back at him.

The door to the kitchen swung open and Oliver emerged balancing three plates on each arm. He took one look at the squabbling trio and barked, 'This is no time for socialising, Kai!'

'Got to go!' said Kai. 'Wait for me, Jen. Please.'

'Why should she?' replied Ellie.

Jen gritted her teeth. 'What time do you finish?'

'I dunno!" He gestured at the full tables.

'Not good enough, babe,' Ellie grabbed Jen by the arm.

'Come on, Jen. I don't know how you put up with him.'

'Shut up!' Jen shrugged off Ellie's hand and turned back to Kai. 'Look, I'll see you tomorrow.'

'No!'

'Kai, you're busy, I can see that. It's no big deal.'

'It is, I don't want you to go.' Kai was beginning to sound desperate. Some of the customers were turning to look at them. 'Stay here and wait for me.'

Ellie groaned. 'I don't believe this. Come on. Let's get out of here.'

Kai looked stricken. 'Where are you going?'

'To the Pass, if you must know,' said Ellie, flouncing out of the door. 'With some guys who know how to have fun.'

Oliver dashed past again and bawled, 'Kai, Table eight are still waiting for their starters. You're on your last warning!'

'Look, give me a ring when you've finished,' said Jen.

'No, wait there!' said Kai urgently. He dashed into the kitchen and reappeared with four plates, balanced precariously. 'I need to speak to you. Just let me get rid of these.'

Jen watched him edging his way through the crowded restaurant. Part of her was moved as usual by his need of her. Part of her was furious with him for confirming all Ellie's prejudices. He was so unreliable.

Maybe Ellie was right after all. Maybe she was a soft touch where Kai was concerned.

Oliver burst out of the kitchen again and glared at her. 'Please go and leave Kai to get on with his job,' he growled.

Jen nodded and turned away. Time to quit. This wasn't doing either of them any good. She hated to leave him like this but she'd had enough. Anyway, he'd end up getting himself the sack if she hung around here any longer.

'See you later, Kai,' she whispered and followed Ellie out of the door.

chapter 8
KAI

Kai dumped the plates down unceremoniously on Table eight and turned around.

He couldn't believe it. She'd gone.

He flung open the door. Ellie was running along the beach towards two guys, her sandals in her hand. Behind her Jen followed more slowly. He narrowed his eyes. One of them was that Aussie lifeguard, Macca. He could tell by his hair.

Kai whipped out his phone and called her. Jen stopped dead and pulled her phone from her pocket. Relief turned to shock as his phone disconnected and Jen walked on to join the others. She'd cut out on him! He watched in disbelief as she caught up with them and continued along the beach towards the Pass.

He felt sick. This was all going so wrong. He should have asked her out there and then. It was too late now, he'd blown it. He looked down at his phone, half-expecting her to call him back, then jealousy turned to fury and he pulled back his arm and hurled it into the sand dunes.

Back inside the restaurant Oliver gave him a filthy look, thrust two more plates at him but refrained from commenting. It was obvious why. Things had heated up and Maggie and Dee were struggling to cope.

Kai threw himself into the fray, whirling from kitchen to table with plates in his hands, biting his tongue at the loud demands and crass comments from the more inebriated diners. Against his better judgement, Oliver had laid on complimentary bottles of wine to make up for the slow service. Unfortunately they weren't having the desired effect: people were becoming rowdier than ever.

In the restaurant all hell was breaking loose. Some guests were clamouring to know when their main courses would be arriving; others had lost all interest in the absent food and were waving empty bottles at him and demanding more. Kai dashed around in circles, trying to remember who'd ordered what.

He was doing his best but this was a total nightmare.

As he made his way to a table with two plates of fresh sea bass in his hands, a big guy stood up and blocked his way. 'What do I have to do to get a drink round here?' he bellowed.

Kai swallowed hard, fighting every instinct to escape. The man, red-faced with drink and temper, led him back to a place he wanted to forget, a place not even Jen knew about. But there was no time to think about that.

38

Kai placed the meals down in front of some waiting customers, grabbed a bottle from behind the bar and opened it up for him.

'Did you put that wine on his bill?' came Oliver's terse voice from behind him.

'I thought it was complimentary,' said Kai, bewildered.

'Not all night long,' said Oliver through gritted teeth. 'And certainly not the most expensive bottle in the house!'

'I'm not paying for this crap,' said the man, knocking it back like water.

'Excuse me. I didn't order the fish. Mine's a steak.' said the man Kai had just served.

'And I'm a Caesar salad,' said the woman.

'I do apologise,' said Oliver in his most charming manner. 'Take these back to the kitchen and fetch a steak for the gentleman and a Caesar salad for the lady.' He picked up the plates, thrust them into Kai's hands and hissed, 'And this time, get it right!'

Kai didn't even know what a Caesar salad looked like. Dizzy with confusion he turned around with the two heaped plates of food and was sent flying by a guy coming out of the Gents. The sea bass shot off the plates and landed on the nearest table, knocking over glasses and showering people in wine.

A big cheer went up around the restaurant.

'That's it,' yelled Oliver. 'You're fired!'

chapter 9

JEN

Jen had seen it was Kai calling her but decided not to answer. There was no point. And anyway, he was going to get himself into big trouble with Oliver if he kept on trying to talk to her. Miserably she'd joined the others heading over to the Pass.

Ellie's incessant chatter to Macca was driving her mad. If she wanted to impress him she was going about it completely the wrong way. She needed to get on a surfboard to do that. It was pretty obvious that was all he was interested in so why couldn't Ellie see it?

To be fair, he was awesome. You could learn a lot just by watching him. Jen stood on the deck above the Pass with Ellie, admiring the way he caught one powerful wave after another, leaping and spinning, crouching and stretching, coaxing the last piece of energy from each one before dropping gracefully into the sea and paddling back out for the next. He was an athlete, a dancer, an acrobat, at home in the water, literally in his element.

She wished she was out there with him. Not because she fancied him – definitely not that. But to be rid of the stuff going round and round in her head. In her heart.

She'd surfed since she was a kid. There was nothing like the sea and a surfboard to sort out your problems.

Kai's not interested in me, Jen acknowledged to herself sadly. Not in that way. I'm just his mate. OK, his best mate. But I'm never going to be any more to him than that.

I'm as bad as Ellie. For the first time that day she felt a twinge of sympathy for her friend, quickly extinguished as Ellie squealed, 'Oh look, Macca and Jay are coming out of the water. Quick! Let's go down and catch them.'

There will always be plenty more fish in the sea for Ellie, she thought sadly. *But not for me. It's Kai I want and nobody else*. Reluctantly, she followed her down the path to the beach.

'That was amazing!' gushed Ellie, running up to Macca.

'Gnarly,' he agreed, shaking the water from his hair like a dog. 'That break handles the southwest swell perfectly.'

'Totally,' nodded Ellie who had no idea what he was talking about.

They hung out on the beach together, the guys talking tactics, Ellie hanging on to their every word. Wondering how soon she could make her escape, Jen lay down on the sand enjoying the evening sun on her face. The guys' low voices were strangely soothing. Before long she could feel herself drifting off . . .

She awoke to find Ellie shaking her.

41

'Come on. We've got to go.'

'Where?' Jen sat up and pushed her hair out of her eyes.

'I've got to babysit, remember? Mum's going to yoga.'

Jen struggled upright. 'So?' Never at her best when disturbed from sleep, she felt dry-mouthed and irritable.

Ellie frowned. 'Aren't you coming? You were snoring by the way.'

'Thanks.' Jen was embarrassed. 'Give me a chance, I've just woken up.'

Ellie glanced at her watch impatiently. 'I've got to go, *now*!'

'Go then,' said Jen grumpily. 'What's keeping you?' What was it Ellie had accused her of? Jumping to Kai's tune? Well, she'd finished with all that. She wasn't going to jump to anyone's tune anymore, least of all Ellie's.

Poor Ellie looked shocked and Jen felt mean. That was a bit harsh. But she was sick to death of being at everyone else's beck and call.

'I don't remember saying I'd come and babysit with you,' she added.

'Stay if you want, Jen,' said Macca. 'I'll walk you home later.'

Ellie's expression changed to fury. 'Jen . . .' she said pointedly, through gritted teeth.

All sympathy Jen had for her vanished. There was no need for her to be jealous. Jen knew Macca didn't mean anything by it, he was just being friendly.

But there was no harm in letting Ellie think he did. She'd had enough of her for one day. She got up and moved over to where Macca was sitting and flopped down beside him.

'Thanks Mac. Might as well,' she said nonchalantly. 'I don't have anything else to be back for.'

chapter 10

KAI

Kai stumbled out of the Beach Café.

He'd blown it. Everything. His job. The big night out. His plan to tell Jen how he really felt about her.

He needed her. He had to explain. He needed to talk to her . . . *now*!

Kai felt in his pocket for his phone then remembered he'd chucked it away. *Idiot*! He scoured the beach frantically, on his hands and knees, but it was nowhere to be seen.

Wondering what the hell to do next he returned to the Beach Café and leant back against the wall. Beside him the restaurant door opened and a man came out. He took a pack of cigarettes from his pocket and offered one to Kai.

'No thanks.'

The man lit up and breathed out a cloud of smoke. 'It's bedlam in there,' he remarked conversationally and when Kai failed to answer he turned to look at him.

'You're the guy who dropped the plates, yeah?'

'Yeah, that's me,' said Kai in a monotone. 'The guy who drops plates.'

'Sorry about that. It was my fault as much as yours.'

Kai glanced sideways. It was him alright, the guy he'd bumped into. He felt a flicker of anger and tried to curb it.

'Don't worry about it.'

He could feel the man studying him curiously. 'D'you know,' he said suddenly, 'you look familiar.'

Kai swung himself away from the wall. 'Gotta go.'

He didn't feel like conversation and anyway, he'd just caught a glimpse of Ellie coming along the path. Thank goodness for that, Jen was bound to be with her.

But when she came fully into view he saw she was on her own.

'Where's Jen?'

'Huh? Good question!' Ellie sounded particularly waspish.

'What do you mean, what's going on?'

'Jen's with Macca, if you must know.'

'What?' Kai's heart dropped like a stone.

'She is! She was supposed to be babysitting with me but she's hanging out with Macca instead. He asked if he could walk her home and she said yes.' Ellie burst into tears. 'How could she?' she wailed. 'I thought she was my friend. She's making a fool of me, and you too.' She stumbled up the hill towards town, sobbing.

Kai watched her go, reeling with shock.

Jen was his friend too. More than his friend.

She was his soul mate. In a weird way he envied Ellie. It was all right for her. She could let go and have a good cry. He couldn't. *Boys don't cry, do they*?

Kai felt his chest grow tight with tension.

'Girl trouble?' The bloke from the restaurant had followed him out and was standing behind him. Kai ignored him.

'You definitely remind me of someone,' he said.

Kai closed his eyes, trying to block him out. *Do you really think this is the time for small talk?*

'What's your name?' he persisted.

Leave me alone jerk or I'm going to smash your face in.

'Listen.' The man was becoming increasingly persistent. 'Is your name Kevin by any chance?'

Something inside Kai snapped and his eyes flew open. He grabbed the man by his shirt collar and threw him up against the wall of the restaurant.

'Do I look like a Kevin?' He banged him back against the wall, once, twice, three times, and shouted in his face, 'My name is Kai, get it? KAI, KAI, KAI!'

Suddenly he let go and found himself charging up the outside stairs of the Beach Café, two steps at a time. He tore along to the end of the balcony and swung himself up onto the rails, peering down at the beach far below.

Just a few people left on it this late in the evening – a couple out for a stroll with a baby in a sling, dogs running for sticks while their owners chatted.

No sign of Jen and Macca. They'd gone.

It was too late. *He* was too late.

He half-turned and his eye caught the table he'd prepared so carefully earlier on. For her. With a mighty roar from somewhere deep inside him, he launched himself on to it. The table and chairs toppled over: cutlery, glasses, flowers, the reserved sign, they all went flying, smashing to the floor. Kicking his way through the mess he'd made, Kai leapt back down the stairs and landed in a heap on the ground.

'What are you doing up there?' Oliver had come out of the restaurant with the bloke Kai had had a go at.

'That's the one.' The man pointed at him. 'I asked him a civil question and he assaulted me!'

'Kai?' said Oliver. 'What the hell is going on?'

Kai got to his feet and pushed them both out of the way.

Oliver swore and charged upstairs to see for himself. Then he swore even louder when he saw what he'd done.

'Kai! Come back here!' he bawled.

But Kai was already off, pelting along the coastal footpath towards home. Oliver and the customer stood and watched him go.

None of them heard Kai's phone vibrating in the sand dunes below.

chapter 11
ELLIE

How could she do this to me?

Ellie sobbed her way up the cliff path towards home, her nose sorely out of joint. It was pretty obvious that Macca was more interested in Jen than her.

Jen had all the luck. First Kai, now Macca. Is this what her life was always going to be like? Doomed to splash around in the shallows while her taller, more confident, *cooler* friend strode the waves, casting her net far and wide to catch all the best guys for miles around?

Probably. She hated the water anyway.

What was wrong with her? Everyone said she was pretty, but it was Jen the boys wanted to be with. It wasn't fair. Jen had a face like a horse.

Only she didn't, did she? Have a face like a horse. That was just her being childish.

Jen had a face like Venus, the goddess of love.

Their art teacher had shown them a picture of Botticelli's

The Birth of Venus and Kai, without thinking, had burst out with, 'That looks just like you, Jen!" in front of everyone. And the whole class had whooped and cheered and fallen about laughing because she was naked. But it was true. Her face looked just like Jen's, all peachy skin and almond eyes and loose, long hair that trailed down past her shoulders. And only Jen could carry it off, laughing with them all, whereas poor Kai's face was bright purple with embarrassment and he looked as if he wanted to run away and hide, which is what he used to do a lot when he was younger, now she came to think of it.

The truth was, Jen might not be conventionally pretty but she was better than that. She was beautiful, inside and out. She was funny and kind and thoughtful and downright, genuinely nice. She was never mean to anyone.

Except her. Just now.

That's what really hurt.

Jen was supposed to be her best friend. And she was hers. Okay, she knew she shared her with Kai, but she'd always felt without doubt that she was Jen's best female friend, which is what counted.

It wasn't just what she'd said which was bad enough. It was the fact that she could do that to her BFF, go off with the boy *she* fancied.

It wasn't fair. She already had Kai. Let's face it, she could have anyone she wanted! So why did she have to have Macca as well? Flirting with him like that when she *knew* Ellie was mad about him.

OK, so maybe Macca wasn't that interested in her yet. But he just needed to get to know her and then he would be. If Jen would get out of his face and give her a chance.

She reached the top of the path, scrubbed at her eyes and took a deep breath. In front of her was the town square where, on Friday nights, everyone met up. Except for her. Tonight she had to go straight home. Her mum was waiting to go out.

'Ellie! Over here! What's wrong?'

Three or four girls from school were hanging out on the benches. She felt her eyes welling up with self-pity again and made her way towards them.

Her mum could wait.

chapter 12

JEN

Jen was beginning to wish she'd gone home with Ellie after all.

OK, she'd been mega annoying. But Macca and Jay were mega boring. Jay had been telling Macca all about Stack Davey, the coxswain of the lifeboat and local legend, who happened to be Jay's personal superhero. To be fair, they were really interesting stories, but Jen had heard them all before.

Now their topic of conversation had turned to surfing, what a surprise. They'd moved on from raving about the virtues of the Pass and were now trying to outdo each other by comparing top spots to surf around the world. She couldn't speak for Macca but she was pretty sure her cousin Jay was beefing his stories up. Like, when had he ever been to Hawaii?

It was a macho boy thing.

Kai wasn't like that. He was the opposite. He never made out he was better than he was. He was quiet and didn't see the need to blow his own trumpet, which was probably why some of the more stupid boys in their year thought he was a wuss.

They were so wrong. There was more than one way to be tough. She'd seen him over the years handle some really difficult situations. Stuff other people knew nothing about.

Actually, there was no way she could have gone back with Ellie. She'd wanted to slap her, making out she was constantly at Kai's beck and call. That's what had started it all.

It wasn't like that. And *she* could talk! Sucking up to Macca all the time.

All the same, Jen felt a bit ashamed. She'd been mean to her friend. She hadn't meant anything by hugging Macca, but when she saw Ellie was jealous she had to admit she'd felt smug. And then one thing had led to another and she'd let her think there was something going on between them.

She remembered how awful she'd felt earlier in the year when Ellie had suddenly started showing interest in Kai. Lucky for Jen, Kai had been totally oblivious to it. He'd blown Ellie out without even noticing she'd been coming on to him. Jen knew she couldn't have stood it if her two best mates had become a couple.

Then other girls had started noticing him too.

But Ellie had every right to fancy him and so did anyone else for that matter. As far as everyone was concerned, Kai was a free agent. She had no one to blame but herself for insisting there was nothing going on between them.

There wasn't.

But she wished there was.

Jen groaned. Her head was going round in circles. This had gone on long enough.

It was time to be honest with Kai. She was going to speak to him once and for all and explain to him exactly how she felt. After all, what did she have to lose? She took out her phone and wandered off down the beach.

Even as she pressed his name she registered that he was probably still at work. His phone would be off. Then it rang and her heart lifted. He must have left already.

When it went to answer phone she was surprised but left a message.

'Kai, have you finished work yet? Give me a call when you do.'

Why hadn't he rung her?

'I'm going to the café to meet Kai,' she announced, walking back to the others.

'We'll walk up with you,' said Jay springing to his feet. 'We're off to town.'

The three of them walked back along the beach. When they came to the café, Jen hesitated. Through the glass door she could see it was heaving inside. Kai must still be at work after all.

There was no point in waiting for him. Disappointed, she began to follow the others up the hill towards town. Then behind her she heard the clinking and clashing of bottles being emptied into a bin and turned round to catch a glimpse of Dee at the back door of the café.

'Busy night, yeah?' she called down to her.

'You're not kidding!' came Dee's weary voice. 'I'm shattered.'

'Is Kai nearly finished?' she asked hopefully. There was a moment's silence.

'Kai left some time ago, love,' said Dee and disappeared back inside the café.

chapter 13
KAI

Kai's lungs felt like they were about to burst. At last he slowed down to a stop and bent over, gulping for air. Sweat dripped off him and a long drool of spittle leaked from his mouth on to the cliff path. Gross. After a while he straightened up and stared at the sky above, taking deep, raw breaths.

His chest hurt.

Good. It took his mind off how upset he was.

He'd blown it. Big time. He'd lost his job, his phone, smashed-up the best table on the balcony and assaulted a customer.

But all of these were nothing compared to losing Jen.

He'd left it too late. She was with Macca now.

He raked his throat and spat, feeling a perverse sense of satisfaction as his saliva mingled with his sweat and drool on the footpath. Bullseye. He'd run along it from the Beach Café without stopping as though if he was fast enough he could leave all that shit behind.

Idiot! That's what he always did when things went wrong. Ran away.

He'd been doing it all his life.

Kai wiped his mouth with the back of his hand and stared out to sea. His heart was slowing down and, despite everything, the ocean in its glassy perfection was having its usual calming effect on him. If he got a move on he'd just about have enough time to get home, collect his board and get out on the water.

It would make him feel better. It always did.

Not the Pass though. There wasn't enough time to get back there. Anyway, he wasn't in the same league as the guys who surfed there.

Guys like Macca.

Kai could feel the anger reigniting and he broke into a run again before it could consume him. He was just passing the turning to the lighthouse when something caught his eye.

In the front garden of a white-painted cottage, a shed door, not properly secured, swung on its hinges. A glimpse of something inside. Something unremarkable to the uneducated eye, but to him instantly recognisable.

Plain and unassuming but beautifully shaped. A Bruce Palmer, 7-foot, Single Fin Collectible. Pure vintage.

There was only one person he knew who possessed a board like that.

Macca.

Of course! This was Jay's house. And Macca was staying with him. Kai smiled grimly. He'd have forty fits if he thought his precious board was on view for everyone to see.

From behind the cottage Kai could make out the sound of a lawnmower. Someone must have forgotten to lock the shed door after they got it out. Careless . . . any opportunist thief could come along and steal it.

Best shut it. You never know who's about, Kai thought.

So that's what he did.

After he had helped himself to Macca's wetsuit and prize surfboard.

Instead of continuing on the cliff path towards home, Kai turned down the lane towards the lighthouse, the surfboard under his arm. A crow on sentry duty *ark-arked* a cross warning at him from a twisted tree, permanently hunched over by the prevailing westerly wind. Above his head, a buzzard circled silently.

The old surfboard was heavier than his modern one and the wetsuit, draped over his other arm, was awkward to carry. He stopped and looked around. No one about. Quickly he stripped off down to his pants and pulled on the wetsuit. Surprisingly it was quite a good fit. Kai rolled his clothes into a ball and stuffed them into the hedge. He wouldn't be long. He'd have the board back before Macca knew it had ever gone missing.

Not that he cared. Kai scowled. Tit for tat. He might have pinched Macca's prize board but the Australian had literally walked away with something – or someone – infinitely more precious to him.

Kai picked up the board, tucked it under his other arm and continued on down the lane. As the road dipped, the ocean now appeared to be above him hanging from the horizon like a washing line and for a second it threw him, like the world had suddenly become topsy-turvy. Then, as he neared the Point, the road curved upwards and the sea was in its right place again. He could hear it below him, heavy as thunder.

At the lighthouse he hesitated. To the left lay the wide expanse of Sandy Bay and the lure of the Pass. He could change his mind, try it out, show them all what he was made of.

Common sense prevailed and he veered right, towards Porthzellan, and followed the narrow, uneven track down past Crabby's Creek. This was a small inlet named by the locals in honour of an old fisherman who kept his boat there and, true to form, there he was unloading his day's catch.

'Alright?' said Kai, automatically offering him the customary local greeting as he passed. The old man grunted in reply and hardly glanced up.

'Storm brewing, boy,' he growled after him.

Kai, intent on picking his way across the rocks, glanced out to sea and saw a beautiful clear sky. Oblivious to the solid grey clouds banking one on top of the other behind him, his gaze was transfixed by the red orb of the sun.

It was fine. Old misery guts. Kai had no idea what his real name was but Crabby suited him in more ways than one.

Even for a fit, healthy young guy like Kai this shortcut across the rocks to Porthzellan Cove was tricky, especially carrying a surfboard. But he was determined to get there now, having come this far.

A beautiful little cove, Porthzellan was unknown to tourists and not particularly well used by locals simply because it was so inaccessible. A path led along the clifftop but cars had to park on the main road and there was a considerable climb down to the beach across huge granite boulders with sly crevasses that threatened to swallow up nervous clamberers. The odd walker made it there in the hope of catching sight of a grey seal bobbing in the clear blue water, but families, swimmers and surfers tended to bypass it in favour of the larger and far more convenient Sandy Bay, with its lifeguards and ice creams and the added attraction of the Pass.

It was one of Kai's favourite spots on earth, a place he hugged to himself. Not even Jen knew just how much it meant to him.

In those first strange days, when he'd arrived in Cornwall with his mum as a scared little kid all those years ago, it was the place they used to come to. Before he'd started school, been befriended by Jen and settled into normal life, he had dug in the sand and played in the shallows of Porthzellan Cove. He and his mum had licked their wounds on this deserted beach in the remotest corner of the country and, soothed by the scrolling waves and curious seals, they had felt safe and had healed.

It was a place he'd returned to over the years whenever he'd messed up. When he needed to get his head back into gear.

He needed it now more than he'd ever done. Losing Jen and the subsequent rage that had engulfed him had frightened him more than words could say.

But tonight he wasn't going to stay on the beach.

Tonight he was going to take the surfboard and paddle out to the sunset.

PART
TWO

chapter 1
KAI

I'm drifting out to sea and nobody knows.

I sit up on the board and stare blankly back at the shore. Through the fading light I can just about make out the old coastguard station and next to it the white coastguard cottages on the cliffs above Porthzellan.

Not much use to me now – they've long been converted to holiday lets.

To the west is a long empty stretch of coast beneath towering cliffs, with the odd house or farm perched on top.

To the east are the lights of Sandy Bay. I can even see the Beach Café.

I wonder if the party is still going on there. I'm pretty sure it will be.

I wonder if Oliver is still mad at me. I'm pretty sure he is.

I wonder if Jen knows I'm missing. I'm pretty sure she hasn't even noticed. She's with Macca. She won't know or care.

This is all her fault. Hers and Macca's. I could die out here and nobody would know! Suddenly it hits me and panic sets in.

'Help!' I shout. 'Help!' The sound reverberates eerily over the water but no one replies. My voice rises to a long, shrill scream. '*H-E-E-E-E-E-E-E-E-L-P!*'

Silence.

Lying on the board, I paddle like crazy for the shore, head down against the buffeting wind, arms thrashing, tearing at the sea. I keep going against the tide for ever, for an age. My arms ache, my chest hurts, my whole body is on fire.

And then it's over. I collapse in a heap on the board, my arms trailing in the water.

I can't do it. I can't do it anymore. My head hurts.

When I look up I'm further out than ever. Beneath me a huge tide is pulling me out to sea and the night is closing in on me.

I am drained, exhausted, frightened.

I want to run away.

But this time I can't.

chapter 2

JEN

What on earth is Kai playing at?

When Dee disappears back into the Beach Café I check my phone.

One missed call, that's all, the one he'd made as soon as I'd left the café. I didn't answer it because I didn't want him to get into more trouble with Oliver. And after that?

Zilch.

No voicemail, no text message, nothing.

I am totally pissed off with him. *Why didn't he call me when he left work?*

I'm about to ring Kai to find out when I stop. *No! Why the bloody hell should I?* He can go and boil his head as far as I'm concerned. Stuffing the phone back in my pocket I follow Jay and Macca up the hill instead. What a crap evening this is turning out to be.

Town is Friday-night busy, especially in the main square where people are spilling in and out of pubs and restaurants.

Everyone congregates here. Half my mates from school are hanging out on the benches, yacking away like mad and, slap-bang in the middle of them, the obvious centre of attention, guess who I spot?

Ellie. I thought she was supposed to be babysitting.

She looks up and her gaze moves from me to Macca and back again. That's when it dawns on me what the hot topic of conversation is.

Me and Macca, an item? I don't think so. Anyway, she doesn't look that upset to me. More like she's loving all the attention.

For a second they all stare goggle-eyed at me, then Ellie gets up and stalks off. One girl, Skyla, the drama queen of our year, runs after her. The rest remain, eager for the next instalment of the story.

'Jen, over here!' Kat stands up and waves to me frantically. Groan. Ceri, Kat and Charley. Three of the biggest gossips around.

Jay grins. 'Uh, oh! Trouble?'

'Fancy a beer?' asks Macca, totally oblivious to the fact that his and my reputations are being torn to shreds on the bench opposite.

Jay wrinkles his nose, considering. 'Dunno. Best not. Forecast's not good. Could be called out tonight, you never know.' He pulls his RNLI pager out of his pocket and waves it at him. Macca shakes his head. Jay's allegiance to the Lifeboats is legendary.

'Well, I'm off to the Swordfish. There's an ice-cold beer with my name on it waiting for me on the bar.'

'OK, I'll come with you," concedes Jay. 'But I'm on the OJ tonight.'

'That's up to you, mate. See you Jen.'

'See you guys.'

You have to laugh. So much for Macca fancying me. My company or a cold beer? No competition. *Ellie, believe me, you have nothing to worry about.*

Nevertheless, I make my way over to the bench feeling like I'm about to be thrown to the lions. They fall over each other to make room for me, practically licking their lips with anticipation, and then they pounce.

'Is it true you're with Macca now?' asks Kat.

I roll my eyes.

'Duh! Do I look as if I'm with Macca? I'm pretty sure I just saw him and Jay disappearing into the Swordfish together.'

'Well, Ellie says you are!' yelps Ceri.

'Doesn't make it true.'

Her nose is practically quivering with curiosity. 'So, what's happened to Kai?'

'Nothing's happened to Kai, as far as I know. I don't even know where he is. You tell me.'

'Dunno. No one's seen him. Ellie said you'd dumped him.'

'I'm not even going out with Kai. How could I dump him?'

'But Ellie said . . .'

'Ellie said! Ellie said!' Poor Ceri jumps as my pent-up frustration erupts. 'It's all in Ellie's head. Listen! Let me spell it out for you, once and for all. I DO NOT FANCY MACCA. NOT ONE LITTLE BIT! Ellie does. I don't. Get it?'

Everyone looks disappointed.

'So where's Kai?' persists Charley.

'*GRRRRR!* How the hell should I know? I'm not his bloody keeper!' I jump to my feet. 'I've had enough of this. I'm off.'

chapter 3
ELLIE

I didn't mean to start crying. And I definitely hadn't meant to bad-mouth Jen to everyone. But it had turned out to be such a rotten evening and they were so understanding – Kat, Ceri, Charley, Skyla, all of them. Especially Skyla.

'You poor thing!' she'd said, putting her arm round me, and I found myself sobbing into her shoulder.

'I thought she was my best friend,' I moan, basking in her sympathy even though I knew she was getting off on this. Everyone knows she can be a right stirrer.

'I can't believe Jen would do that to you,' says Ceri.

'I can,' retorts Skyla snidely. 'I wouldn't trust her as far as I could throw her.'

Wow! That's a bit harsh! In that case, asks the rational part of me beneath the tears, *why are you always jumping around Jen's ankles like an irritating little dog, Skyla, wanting to be her friend?*

'It's obvious how much you like Macca,' said Charley, who likes him too.

'I thought Jen and Kai were a couple,' says Ceri. 'Poor Kai. You wait till he finds out. He's going to be gutted.'

'They've been joined at the hip since the infants,' agrees Kat. 'Fancy Macca having the neck to ask her out in front of you.'

'And she agreed!' says Charley in wonder. 'I can't believe it.'

I bite my lip and say nothing even though it hadn't been quite like that. It felt good to be the centre of attention at last after I'd been side-lined all evening by Jen. She and Kai had more or less told me to get lost.

'She's a right cow.' announces Skyla sourly. 'Everyone knows what Jen wants, Jen gets.'

That was so untrue. Jen wasn't a bit like that.

Skyla's jealous of Jen. She wanted the lead part in the school show and Jen got it. And now I come to think of it, earlier this year Skyla was one of those, like me, who'd suddenly noticed that Kai was actually quite cool. Needless to say he'd been blind to us all. He only had eyes for Jen.

I feel a pang of guilt and find myself studying my shoes.

'She could have anyone she wants,' remarks Ceri, wistfully.

'Yeah, she could,' agrees Kat, which does nothing for my ego.

'She thinks she's better than the rest of us,' adds Skyla maliciously, and even though I'm mad at Jen, I know this simply isn't true. Jen is the least vain person I know, and the least selfish. That's how all this fuss had started in the first place; the fact that she was hanging around at the café worrying about Kai when I was desperate to be on the beach with Macca.

This was all growing out of control; I have to stop it now. I take a deep breath, look up and open my mouth to put them straight.

And that's when I see them, opposite me, on the other side of the square. Jen and Macca. Together. Plus the nice lifeguard Jay, her cousin.

She's staring at me. And I can tell by the expression on her face exactly what she's thinking. *What's she hanging out with that bunch of losers for?*

I spring to my feet and march off.

Skyla follows me.

chapter 4
KAI

It's getting dark now. I wonder what time it is.

Dark and cold. The wind has whipped up and the sea is choppy.

Huge clouds have smothered the sky and snuffed out the rising moon. The ocean is vast. If I face out to sea it's endless. If I turn the other way I can still see the lights of Sandy Bay, though they're further away now.

The wind is offshore. It's taking me further and further out and there is nothing I can do about it. When I sit up I am shocked by its force. Bile rises into my throat as panic seizes me. I need to get back.

What should I do?

Swim for it.

What would Jen do?

Why am I thinking about her? She doesn't care about me.

Nevertheless, I know what she'd say. 'Stupid idea. Sit tight and wait to be rescued.'

I can hear her voice as clearly as if she's out here with me. That bang on the head has knocked me silly. Every surfer knows if you get into difficulties in the sea the first rule of thumb is, never leave your board.

I do as I'm told, check my leash is secure and drop back down flat.

But nobody knows you're out here, says the insidious little voice inside my own head. *You could die of hypothermia out here waiting to be rescued. Do it while you've got the chance.*

Shut up! Listen to Jen. So long as I stay with my board I'll be fine. Someone will come. I've just got to wait.

I'm shivering. I feel sick.

There's a noise above me. A growl and it's getting louder.

My heart lifts. A rescue helicopter. *Already?*

I sit upright and search the sky but the clouds blot everything out. The noise recedes and I'm gutted. Then it comes back only now it's directly overhead. The growl turns into a thunderclap and I realise there is no helicopter. Thunder reverberates from the sky which flickers like a dodgy light bulb and suddenly rain is lashing down on me in painful, biting bullets.

Within minutes, all around me the sea is rising and falling, surging and seething. Hurling myself flat, I grip the edges of my board and hang on grimly, rigid with effort, as the ocean churns and boils, intent on unseating me and dragging me into its depths. It's like being trapped inside an evil washing machine that wants to twist me and tangle me and drain all the life from me.

As the wind gusts and howls, thunder roars and crashes, and lightning forks its way across the sky. The sea around me lights up briefly in jagged silver streaks and I scream my defiance to the elements.

'NOOOOOOOOOOOOOOOOOOOOOOOOOO!'

But no one is listening.

chapter 5

JEN

As I head for home I notice that it's already beginning to get dark. Not only has the sun set but big clouds are gathering and the wind is really strong. I'm glad Jay and Macca are not still out on the water. Jay was right. The weather is changing fast.

There's a crash of thunder and a flash of lightning out at sea. Soon the rain is chucking it down and I start to run. Good job, I think meanly. Ellie and the others will get drenched.

But by the time I make it to my front door it's me who's soaked to the skin. *Serves me right.*

I hope Kai's safe and dry somewhere and out of the rain. I check my phone again but there's nothing. *Stuff him!*

When I walk through the door, Mum is lying on the sofa, watching her favourite soap on catch-up TV with a large glass of red wine and a bowl of veggie crisps. She's always the same, on Friday nights she literally likes to veg out. She works in customer relations for a local renewable energy firm, and by the end of the week she doesn't want to talk to anyone.

'Where's Dad?' I ask, trying to make conversation.

'Pub.'

'Adam?'

'Taekwondo. Then sleepover at Toby's.'

Her eyes don't leave the television.

'Anything to eat?'

'Kitchen.'

'It's pouring down out there. I'm soaked through.'

She doesn't respond. I'm standing in front of her like a drowned rat but she hasn't even noticed. Hoping I'll take the hint, she leans forward, picks up the remote and turns the volume up. She couldn't make it plainer if she tried. *Go away!*

I wander off to the kitchen and start eating the dried-up remains of tonight's supper: shepherd's pie, straight from the dish. Yum. Not. My evening just gets better and better.

Friday night, no one to talk to, nothing to do.

It's all Kai's fault.

But all the same, I can't help wondering where he's got to.

I feel a bit lost without him.

chapter 6

KAI

It's pitch dark now and freezing cold.

Lying on my board, cheek pressed flat against it, I'm totally knackered and shivering uncontrollably.

But inside a small flame of satisfaction is licking me back to warmth.

The worst place in the world to be when lightning strikes is on the open sea. But I did it. I got away with it. I ran with the wind.

It had changed again, suddenly, blowing up from behind. Quickly I had seized my chance, pointing the nose of the board into a wave and ploughing through it safely. Again I did it, again and again, and now the sea was a roller coaster and I was up and down, twisting and turning with the waves and '*JE-SUS!*' I screamed, each time.

And finally, I rode out those waves, away from the path of the storm into calm waters.

Me, who's never even ridden the Pass. No one would ever believe me. I can't be far from shore now.

Only, when I lift my head I see with a shock that I'm further out than I was before. I can't see the lights of Sandy Bay anymore.

And I realise that I didn't outrun the storm after all. It outran me.

Where am I? Have I drifted along the coast? I scramble up and groan. I have no idea. I'm no longer even sure which way I'm facing. I swivel around on the board, peering this way and that but all I can see is vast inky blackness and I feel panic rising inside me.

I'm all alone.

'Serves you right for blaspheming,' comes a voice. It's Jen's. She's laughing at me and it's like she's on the board right next to me, though I can't see her. Her voice grounds me.

'I'm not sure I was,' I answer aloud. 'What should I do then? Swim for it?'

'Don't be an idiot. You know better than that. I told you, stay with your board. We'll find you.'

'It's not my board. It's Macca's.'

She laughs again.

I pat the board and find myself grinning. I wonder if he's discovered it's missing yet?

It won't be long now. They'll come and find me soon. Jen's right. Stay with the board.

I need to rest. Keep my strength up while I'm waiting. I lie down again.

It's almost still now, the sea barely lapping beneath me. I feel like I'm in a cradle, being gently rocked to sleep. My eyes close and my brain switches off . . .

I'm back surfing the waves again only this time I'm standing up. They lift me to the crest and bear me back down again on the other side. And they're all watching . . . Macca, Jay, Danny, Ben . . . all of them . . . and so are the kids in my class and they're cheering me on . . .

I'm surfing properly. I'm trimming, gliding, slicing across waves, walking to the front of the board and back again. My feet cross over each other in precise, elegant steps, adjusting to each wave as it steeps and flows beneath me.

I can do this. I'm actually cross-stepping. I'm dancing.

I curl my toes, all ten of them, around its nose and I've never done this before in my life but it's easy. I'm soaring into the air . . . I'm leaping from one wave to another . . .

I'm flying!

. . . and then, in my sleep, I fall off my board into the freezing depths of the ocean and am swallowed up.

chapter 7
JEN

My phone is silent.

At least the downpour has made everyone go home so there's not a million annoying photos on Facebook of everyone else out enjoying themselves. There's nothing worse than watching people having fun when you're not.

I troll through Ellie's posts but there's nothing new. Thank goodness for that. To be fair, she might go for the private sympathy vote from our mates but I don't think she'd diss me online for all to see.

There's no point in cyber-stalking Kai. He's the one fifteen year old in the world who doesn't have an internet presence. His phone is just that, for basic calls and texts, an old pay-as-you-go with no lock on it. They don't even have a computer at home. Or a TV.

I guess that's why Kai's like he is. Different. In a world of his own.

Like his mum. They're so isolated, just the two of them out there in that tumbledown cottage on the cliffs. I used to find her a bit odd years ago when I played with Kai as a kid. It was like Kai was looking after her, not the other way round. Looking back, I reckon half the time she was off her head on weed or booze.

Though, she's got her act together now, to be fair. She's gone all arty-crafty and sells her stuff in a café in town. But Kai says she won't sell it online. Weird. Everyone knows that's the easiest way to make a business work these days.

I haven't been out to Kai's place for ages. We tend to hang out in Sandy Bay nowadays.

Where is he? I miss him. I miss the way his hair flops in his eyes and his crooked grin and the way he chews the skin around his thumbnail when he's concentrating. And the way he makes me laugh.

This is stupid.

I press his number. It rings and rings, then goes to answer phone.

chapter 8
ELLIE

What a horrible night it's been.

I'd been on the point of telling them all, Ceri and that lot, that it wasn't true. I'd exaggerated. If I'm honest with myself I know that Jen hadn't really got off with Macca. She'd just stayed on the beach with him and Jay because she didn't want to come home with me.

Then I looked up and saw her staring at me across the square in that way of hers and I could tell she knew what we'd been talking about. And I just knew she'd be doing that disapproving little headshake she does when people are being immature even though I was too far away to see it.

Because she's *so* mature isn't she? Not like me. I feel like a kid beside her sometimes, even though we're the same age and she's my best friend.

But I'm not her best friend, am I? Kai is and I'm just the hanger-on.

That's what the real trouble is. It's not that Kai fancies her more than me. Though actually, that is a bit annoying. A lot annoying, to be honest. He doesn't even see me, or anyone else for that matter. He's only got eyes for Jen.

Imagine someone being that besotted with you? I wonder if anyone will ever like me as much . . .

No, what really gets me is the fact that Kai is closer to her than I'll ever be. It's like he takes up all her attention. She'd much rather be with him than with me. She made that so obvious today.

I didn't mean to lie to the others. Actually, I didn't lie. Macca did say he'd walk her home and she said OK, but it wasn't like that. And I forgot to mention that her cousin Jay was there, too. And then it all blew up out of proportion like things do. Especially if Skyla's around.

Now they'll all hate me. Jen, Macca and Jay.

And it's pouring down and I'm getting wet.

And when I get home I'm going to get it in the neck from my mum for being late for babysitting.

One consolation.

At least Skyla disappeared as soon as it started raining.

chapter 9

KAI

No sooner am I submerged, than I'm wide awake and scrambling up again, as fast as I can, my lungs bursting. I break through the surface, hawking like a seal.

Where is it? I turn round in rapid circles of terror. *Where is my board?*

I feel a sharp tug on my ankle and remember, thank God, I am leashed to it. It jerks away and I strike out in that direction and in the darkness my arm smacks down hard on it. I grab it and the board turns over and I have to turn it back on its right side.

Somehow, I don't know how, I find the strength to haul myself up on to it and then I collapse, wheezing and choking. I lie flat, heart racing, chest and abdomen heaving, my eyes open-wide. NEVER will I close them again, come hell or high water.

Come hell or high water. I know what that phrase means now. I've got to stay awake till I'm back on dry land.

'Back on dry land,' I whisper, longingly. The sound of a voice, even mine, in this immense, infinite darkness, is comforting. Gradually my heart slows down.

Keep awake.

I need someone to talk to.

Talk to yourself.

'What about?'

Anything.

'OK. I'm freezing.'

You're not kidding. A chattery bite, that's what you need.

'A chattery bite? Where did that come from?' My mind struggles to recall the phrase from the forgotten mists of childhood.

Mum used to give you them when you were little, remember? When you came out of the sea at Porthzellan. Your knees would be knocking with the cold and your teeth chattering, clickety-clack, clickety-clack . . .

'. . . and she'd give me a chattery bite! Something to eat to warm me up. Like a sandwich. Or a pasty if I was lucky.'

I wish I had a chattery bite to warm me up now.

I lie in a straight line shivering, my cheek stuck to the board, arms pressed against my sides, trying to conserve the little warmth I have, and think about those early days in Cornwall. We'd got off the train at the end of the line, as far as we could go, and stayed in a caravan in a farmer's field.

Then we'd discovered Porthzellan, a magical playground of caves and rock pools, sand and scrolling waves. Long days were spent there: sunny days, cloudy days, even grey, mizzly days, full of Cornish mist and drizzle.

'Skin's waterproof,' said Mum, but she'd put my plastic mac in for me, just in case.

Before long the summer holidays were over and the families disappeared back to their homes and schools. Not us, though. We stayed on. Then it was just her and me on that beach and an old whiskery seal who used to poke his head out of the sea and watch us.

'He's on guard,' Mum would say. 'Like a policeman. Making sure we're safe.'

Safe from what?

Silence, except for the sound of the sea, lapping against my board.

I had long hair then, past my shoulders, like Mum's. Like a girl. I used to hide behind it.

Hide from what?

Don't think about it.

It hadn't always been long. Suddenly I can clearly recall a younger self. I don't know why, perhaps it's the sensation of the sea rocking me gently. But I'm not a baby, I'm a toddler, or a bit older than that, maybe. I have a vivid sensation of being chucked up in the air and being caught by a pair of strong arms and there's no hair hanging over my face. I'm open. I'm laughing. He's laughing. It's fun.

'More!' I shout.

'Kevvy, Kevvy, Kevvy, Kevvy, Kevin,' repeats the man and rubs his cheek against mine, holding me tight. His face is big and stubbly and mine is small and soft, and I screech with pleasure and lock my hands into his thick, dark hair, tugging it hard.

'Ouch!' he shouts. 'Now you're for it.' And he chucks me up in the air again and I'm chuckling, fit to burst.

'Were there two of us then?' I blurt out loud.

What d'you mean? I've startled myself. Where did that come from? *There's not really two of us. You're just talking to yourself to keep yourself awake.*

'I know that. But in those days, when I was a little kid, was there another boy?'

Don't be daft. There's only ever been you.

'So who's Kevin?'

chapter 10

JEN

Where is he?

I stare out of my bedroom window at the awful weather. The sky is black over the bay. I bet it's lashing it down out at sea. You wouldn't want to be out there on a night like this.

I call him again.

Why isn't he answering? It's not like Kai to sulk. Yeah, he can be a bit moody if something is worrying him – and let's face it, he's had good cause over the years, the state his mum used to get in – and he's got a bit of a temper, but it's over in a flash.

It's like he scares himself more than anyone else. I've seen him struggling hard to control it. He'll run off if something is getting to him, which drives me mad.

He's done so well at the Beach Café. Proved himself to be reliable for once, whatever Ellie says. He's even talking about Oliver training him up to be a chef. That's why I didn't want him to mess up tonight. That's why I didn't answer his call.

I wonder if that's what's upset him? Maybe he thinks I don't care.

What's wrong, Kai? What is it?

I'm always here if you need me. You know that.

I press his number once more.

Pick up Kai. Pick up.

But there's no reply.

chapter 11

KAI

First sign of madness, so they say. Talking to yourself.

I've never been a bletherer, me. 'Keep things to yourself,' Mum used to warn me. 'Our business is nobody's but our own.' So I did. All my life. And now everyone thinks I'm quiet. And weird.

Except Jen.

I talk to her. Loads.

You don't tell her everything though.

'Go away, you. I'm not talking to you anymore.'

I feel warmer now. Or at least, my teeth have stopped chattering and I'm no longer shivering. I'm drifting, drifting, drifting. My eyelids are heavy.

It's peaceful out here. I could go to sleep and when I wake up this nightmare would all be over.

'Don't fall asleep!' a voice reminds me. It's Jen. She's back again. I raise my head.

'I'm here.'

I turn and this time I can actually see her. She's behind me, hanging on to the back of my board, her long hair plastered to her shoulders. Surreal.

'Did you swim here?' I ask in surprise but she disappears then pops up in front of me, treading water. 'What are you? A mermaid?'

'Don't be daft. I'm always here if you need me, you know that.'

It's true. She is. Why did I ever doubt her? That's what got me into this mess in the first place.

'Budge up.' She scrambles up and the board rocks alarmingly. She tosses her head and droplets fall back into the water in a perfect sparkling crescent. Her jeans and t-shirt cling to her body. She's beautiful. Venus, rising from the sea.

'You've got to stay awake,' she says matter-of-factly, 'or you'll die.'

'To die, to sleep . . .' I murmur.

'Kai!' she says warningly. 'I mean it, sit up!'

I do as I'm told, reluctantly. She's right, as usual. There's a breeze. Sitting up, I feel colder but more alert.

'Now then, listen to me.' she says urgently. 'No more talk of dying and sleeping, OK? You're not going to die on my watch, not if I've got anything to do with it.'

I laugh, despite myself. 'It's a quotation, idiot!'

Her face clears. 'I might have known it. Where from?'

'Shakespeare? We did it in year ten, remember? Hamlet's famous soliloquy.'

91

'Oh, yeah. The one where he's contemplating suicide. Don't even think about it, Kai.'

'I'm not.'

'And I'm not thick. I just didn't learn chunks of it like you did. Nerd.'

She grins at me. She doesn't mean it. I know it's one of the things she likes about me, my love of words. Strange passion for someone who doesn't say a lot. It's like they're all bottled up inside me. Jen knows though. I read her stuff I like, poems and that, and recite my favourites off by heart. I write them as well.

But I don't show her the ones about her.

'How does it go? "*To be or not to be; that is the question.*" See? I do know it,' she says triumphantly.

'What comes next?'

"*Whether 'tis nobler in the mind . . . to suffer the*" . . . blah, blah, blah de blah . . . I dunno!'

I pick it up.

'. . . *slings and arrows of outrageous fortune,*

Or to take arms against a sea of troubles,

And by opposing end them.'

'Show-off!' she announces, then grins at me mischievously. '*You're* in a sea of troubles!'

'I am, aren't I?' But now she's here it doesn't seem so bad.

'*To die, to sleep . . .*' I continue . . .

'Don't you dare, Kai!' she says warningly. 'I'm watching you. Just hang in there.'

But her voice is fading away and so is she. A pool of silvery light appears in front of my board where she was and I glance up at the sky in surprise. The clouds are breaking up and the edge of the moon is peeping down at me.

It's OK, Jen. You've got nothing to worry about.

Poor old Hamlet. He probably wasn't that much older than me but he'd had enough of this weary world. He wanted to end his life. He wanted to fall asleep and die, poor guy.

I don't. I've hardly begun my life yet.

I want to stay awake and live.

chapter 12
JEN

In the end I ring Ellie.

At first I think she's not going to pick up either but eventually she does. Ellie can't resist a phone call.

'Yes?' Her voice is cold. She's still mad at me.

'Ellie, I don't know where Kai is.' I blurt out.

'So?'

'I didn't mean to say it like that. I meant to say sorry for being so horrible to you. But the truth is, I don't like Macca, not in that way, but I do like Kai, and Ellie, I haven't a clue where he is!'

She hears the panic in my voice. It surprises me too.

'Jen, slow down! What's happened?'

'I dunno! I went back to the café to meet him but he'd gone. I've been trying to get hold of him all night but he's not answering.'

It sounds a bit feeble now I've put it into words. What is there to get in a tizz about? But to my surprise Ellie takes it seriously.

'That's not like Kai, playing hard to get. Not with you, anyway. Have you tried his house number?'

'No.' How stupid am I? We're so used to using our mobiles. 'You haven't seen him then?' I add hopefully.

'Nope. Look, Jen, I'm sure he's fine. You saw how busy it was in there. He's probably gone home for a kip.'

'But that's the point. It was still crazy when I went back. So why did he leave?'

She clears her throat. 'I hate to say this, but you know what he's like. Maybe he couldn't handle it and decided to leg it.'

'But why didn't he ring me?'

'Look, I don't know. Give him a call on his house phone and find out.'

'OK. You're right. Thanks, Ellie.'

Silence. Then she says kindly, 'Jen, I'm sure he'll be OK. I'd come round and keep you company till he turns up but my mum's still out and I can't leave the kids. Let me know how you get on, right?'

'I will.' I feel better already now that I'm back on speaking terms with her.

Then she adds, 'Oh, and Jen? Well done for finally admitting that you and Kai are more than just mates.'

I hesitate, about to deny it from force of habit, then I hear myself whisper, 'I do like him, Ellie. I really, really do.'

'Course you do,' she says kindly. 'And he really likes you. More than likes you. It's blindingly obvious to everyone except you and Kai that you are both totally bonkers about each other. Now can you ring him up and tell him please and put us all out of our misery!'

She's right. Buoyed by Ellie's fabulous acceptance of the obvious, I call his house phone. His mum answers.

'Hi, it's Jen. Can I speak to Kai please?'

There's a moment of silence.

Then she says, 'But he's not here, Jen. I thought he was with you.'

chapter 13
KAI

As the clouds disperse, the moon appears. It's huge.

Of course. It's a full moon. I'd forgotten, hidden away as it was behind the clouds. Full moon, spring tide. I should've thought.

I used to think spring tides came in the spring but it's nothing to do with the time of year, it's to do with the moon. Spring tides are very strong.

Now I can see how far I have drifted from shore. In the distance I can just about make out the blink of the lighthouse, pinpricks of individual buildings, the ribbon of light of Sandy Bay and to the east the fuzzy blur of a bigger town further up the coast. Not much else.

The wind has dropped and the sea is gentle now. The swell no longer running in all directions but replaced by a steady rocking motion – up, down, up, down – that lulls me into calmness.

Don't go to sleep! I tell myself. *Jen's watching you.*

Kai means Ocean in Hawaiian, did you know that? And Jen means White Wave. How ironic is that? I guess we were always meant to be together.

I looked up our names online at school the other day. Then I googled the Birth of Venus, because she's the spitting image of Jen, and got done by the librarian for perving at nude pictures.

'It's art, not porn,' I'd protested, 'It's Botticelli!'

'And I'm Brenda Battersby and these are my computers!' she'd countered, and banned me from using them.

I allow myself to drift for a while, chin on my hands, watching the lights and reflecting on the unfairness of life. As the penny drops that there is no longer any possible chance I can make it back to shore by myself, I realise that I am no longer afraid.

I am here. I'm alive. It's enough.

You know what you have to do, Kai, I tell myself sternly. *It's not rocket science. Stay awake and stay with your board. That's all. The rest is not up to you.*

People will be looking for you by now, wondering where you've got to. It won't take them long to work out what's happened.

Then I curse aloud as I remember that I'm not on my own board. They won't have a clue I'm out at sea.

'Stop it!' I tell myself sternly. 'Stop panicking. It won't be long before Macca realises his precious board is missing. Then they'll come looking for you.'

I heave a huge sigh. I'm glad I'm on this big beauty, not mine, it's far more stable. *Thanks Macca. And thanks for your wetsuit too. Jen said the other guys took the piss out of you about the extra-thick suit you wore to protect your delicate Aussie flesh from the cold waters of an English summer.*

Well, I'm not laughing mate, just grateful. It's tons better quality than mine. My body feels fine. I just wish it had a hood on it. My head's cold. And my hands and feet.

Bloody hell! You know what that means!

Hypothermia!

My eyes open wide and I shoot upright, my legs in the water. My body is diverting its warmth away from the extremities to my vital organs.

Calm down. It's keeping your heart pumping, your lungs breathing and your kidneys functioning. It's doing what it's supposed to do. You'll be fine, your fingers and toes are not going to drop off. I don't think so anyway. What's the sea temperature, 10 degrees? You don't get frostbite in that, do you? All you have to do is hang on and concentrate on conserving your energy till help arrives.

I'm proud of myself. I sound like Jen.

And then it happens.

I'm about to lie prone again when I feel something in the sea, nudging my leg. I scream and pull them both out of the water in a flash and sit upright on the bones of my arse, hugging my knees.

Shark Alert! One or two had been spotted off the coast last summer. It looks like they're back.

My heart is racing again like I'm running for my life. And I'm shivering, but this time with fear, and I'm peering into the inky blackness of the ocean, searching, searching, searching, but terrified of what I might find.

And then I spot it, under the water.

A long, cylindrical shape is circling my board. I knew it! It's a big one! I can't make out its head but I know, without a shadow of a doubt, that it's watching me, watching it.

We stay like that for a timeless moment then suddenly it swoops beneath me.

The board flips up and over me and I pitch backwards like a gymnast into the sea.

chapter 14

JEN

Oh no!

Now I get it. 'Wait for me.' and 'Don't go.' and 'I need to speak to you.'

It wasn't Kai being awkward or needy like Ellie made out. I should have ignored her. I should have had more faith in him.

It was because he'd planned a big surprise for me.

His mum told me. She thought we were at the Beach Café. Apparently, Kai had arranged a special meal for us tonight on the balcony overlooking the sea. He knows how much I've always wanted to eat out there.

'But why?' I ask. 'It's not my birthday.' I'm confused. *What was it for?*

Silence again. Then, 'You'd better ask Kai.'

So I was wrong. I don't really know what this was about at all. I just know that I've messed up big time. Kai had planned this treat for me and I'd bailed out on him.

Treat? What am I saying? It sounded more like a date.

I feel terrible. 'Have you any idea where he could be? He's not answering my calls.'

'I don't know, Jen.'

I bet she hates me now. She and Kai are pretty close.

'Look, I need to speak to him. I had no idea he was planning this. Would you ring him for me? *Please?* He won't talk to me but he'll answer you.' I sound desperate but I don't care. 'Can you tell him I'm really, really sorry?'

'I can try.' Her voice is gentle and reassuring. 'Don't worry love, I'm sure everything's fine. I'll call you right back.'

I don't deserve her kindness. I sit there in the silence of my bedroom, biting my nails, counting the passing of time by the periodic wailing of the same old theme tune from the TV downstairs. Episode four? Five? Mum is lost in *Coronation Street*, totally oblivious to the real-life drama unfolding upstairs.

At last my phone rings and I grab it. It's her.

'You're right,' she says. "Kai's not picking up. I called three times in a row. It's not like him.' She sounds concerned. 'Jen? I have to ask . . . did you two have a row?'

I lick my lips nervously. 'Not a row, exactly. The café was really manic. He had to work on. He wanted me to wait but Oliver was getting cross so I left. I didn't know!'

'That's where he'll be then, at the Beach Café.' Her voice is light with relief.

'No, you don't understand! I went back, but he'd gone. Dee told me. But I don't know why, it was still busy in there.'

102

'Knowing him, he must've walked out.' Her voice flat now, foreboding, cuts through my frantic thoughts. 'Something will have upset him.'

She's right. He was already in a state when I'd left. That's exactly what he would do. I have this awful feeling that it's all my fault.

A bleeping sound interrupts us. I've got an incoming call. 'Just a sec!'

It's him! Thank goodness for that.

'It's okay,' I say. 'He's on the line. I'll call you back!'

'No problem. ' I hear the amusement in her voice. And the relief. I feel it too. I swipe his picture and shout, 'Kai! Where are you? I'm freaking out here, not knowing where you've got to.'

There's silence at the other end. He must think I've gone loopy. This is not a bit like me.

'Kai?'

A cough. A cold tendril of fear curls itself around my heart. I never knew till this second that you could recognise someone – or not – from the way they cleared their throat.

'Who is this?'

'I've just found this phone.' A woman's voice. 'I wanted to return it to its rightful owner and your number was listed under ICE.'

ICE? Then it dawns on me, 'In Case of Emergency'. Kai had listed my name as his emergency contact. The tendril tightens its grip.

'Where did you find it?' I ask weakly.

'Sandy Bay. It was in the sand dunes not far from the Beach Café.'

I close my eyes. *What the hell has happened to him?* I try to gather my thoughts. 'It's my boyfriend's.' *Where did that come from?* 'He must've dropped it. Is the café still open?'

'Yes, I think so. The lights are on.'

'Could you hand it in there please? And tell the manager that it's Kai's and Jen is on her way to pick it up. And thanks. Thanks a lot.'

I press end, take a deep breath, and call Ellie. She's still babysitting but fair play to her, she offers to phone around to find out if anyone's seen Kai while I leg it down to the Beach Café.

I slip out without telling Mum. I shouldn't be long. It's dark now but at least the rain's stopped. When I get to the café the lights are still on but the door is locked. I hammer on it and am rewarded by a shout of, 'We're closed!'

'Oliver, it's me, Jen. Let me in. I've come to collect Kai's phone.'

There's the sound of a bolt being drawn back and a grim-faced Oliver appears and slaps the phone into my hand. 'You can tell your boyfriend from me that I'll be sending him a bill for criminal damage. He's fired by the way.'

'What?' I'm stunned. 'What's been going on?'

'He was worse than useless on shift this evening. In the end I told him to go. And then he kicked off big time – ended the night by smashing up a table.'

'Kai?' I can't believe my ears. 'He wouldn't do that!'

'Oh believe me, he did. Oh yeah, and he assaulted a customer as well.'

'What?' I'm totally bewildered. 'But why would he do that? He loved this job . . .'

'Not tonight, he didn't. His mind wasn't on the game. He needed to step up and instead he was a bloody liability! I need people I can rely on.'

You can tell Oliver is upset. They've always got on so well. I stare at him sadly and say, 'Kai's never served in the restaurant before. He wasn't even meant to be working tonight. He was doing you a favour.' Oliver looks a bit uncomfortable. 'His mum's just told me that he'd booked us a table on the balcony. It was meant to be a surprise for me.

Oliver slapped his hand to his brow. 'So he did! I'd forgotten. It was so hectic . . .'

'Was that the table he smashed up? The one we were meant to have dinner on?'

'Yep.' Oliver groans. 'Bloody hell. Where is he now?'

I stare at him miserably.

'I haven't a clue.'

chapter 15
KAI

I come up, coughing and spluttering, and yelp in terror as something grabs at my ankle.

I try to break away but it won't let me go.

It's my leash.

Relief surges through me momentarily then the shark brushes past and I'm screaming, my arms thrashing around like a windmill. From the corner of my eye I spot my board and like a flash – one, two, three strokes – I'm there, pulling myself up. I'm terrified it's going to grab me by the leg, snap it off in its powerful jaws, pull me back under . . .

And then I've done it. I'm lying on my board, eyes closed, gasping for breath. It's gone. I've beaten off the shark.

Slowly my breathing returns to normal and my eyes open and focus.

I blink. Dread returns. Something is in the sea a few metres away from me, poking out of the water.

A fin?

Cautiously, I raise my head. Wrong shape. *Phew!* It's a small rock, dark and pointy.

Only . . . it's bobbing about a bit, moving a little from side to side. And it's got a face.

I narrow my eyes and study it. Dark eyes with long lashes, staring down its nose at me. A fine nose, a roman one, with big nostrils. An impressive display of whiskers.

It's watching me.

I know that face.

It belongs to a hook-nosed sea pig.

Otherwise known as a grey seal. A big old bull by the look of it.

It could be my very own seal from Porthzellan Cove, making sure I'm safe. Who knows? They all look the same, these old timers, and I've never got this close to one before. But I'd like to think it's him, come to find me.

Either way, it's definitely not a shark.

I feel stupid. I should've known better. The old boy had come to check me out like they do if you're an unknown object close to the surface of the sea, just in case you're a predator like an orca. And then, when he saw I was just some dumb kid on a surfboard he'd got nosy, maybe wanted to play around a bit, but to his surprise I'd freaked out and now, wisely, he's keeping an eye on me from a safe distance.

At least now I've got some idea how far out I am. Seals rarely venture more than a few miles from land.

I read somewhere that sometimes they give their young a ride on their backs in the sea. Maybe he'll give me a ride back home.

'Here boy! Come on, Sammy. Come to Kai.' I click my fingers, then stick them in my mouth and give a piercing whistle like I'm calling a dog.

Sammy the seal. How original is that? He looks at me pityingly, then turns his head away.

I don't blame him. It was a crazy idea. Worth a try though.

It's good having him around, anyway. I don't feel alone anymore.

The cloud has disappeared and, as the sea laps at my board, I turn onto my back and stare up at the moon. It's white and high and full. I can see a face in it. The man in the moon is watching me, watching him. Across the sky, myriads of stars shimmer and sparkle like diamonds.

It's beautiful. How many people actually get to see this?

Fear drops away from me like a discarded coat as I lie there watching the clear night sky with a seal for company, and remember.

chapter 16

MOONSHINE

Many moons ago, in years gone by, a boy and a woman came to live by the sea.

Just the two of them.

They came from another place. And another, before that. And another, before that.

The boy was young. The woman was quite young, too. But she felt old.

They kept themselves to themselves. The woman worked hard and looked after the boy and the boy tried to be good and look after his mother because they loved each other very much.

Once in a blue moon, on a fine summer's night when the world was fast asleep, the woman would wake the boy from his bed and he would follow her, yawning and rubbing his tired, prickly eyes, down the long, winding lane, past the lighthouse and over the rocks, to the sandy beach where the sea rolled and rippled and the waves beckoned.

There they would swim in the moonlight where the land curves round to hold the sea and the sky reaches down to touch the horizon. Through patches of moonshine and dark, silky swatches of cold, clear water, with fish that made room for them and curious seals and even, on one momentous occasion, a pair of dolphins.

In that other world, beneath the ocean, they bathed their life wounds in a sea dance. As they swirled and twirled and pirouetted in the water, shouting their joy to the moon, the salt water cleansed them and fronds of plants and seaweed reached out to brush against them, anointing them with their gentle salve. And gradually they healed, though they would always bear the scars, especially the woman, whose wounds went deeper than the boy's.

But scars fade, like memories, and before long you've forgotten all about them. They're still there though, on the inside.

chapter 17
JEN

I can't sit on my own waiting so after I leave Oliver I go round to Ellie's. Her Mum's back now. Ellie's been ringing around to see if anyone knows where Kai is, but she keeps getting the same answer. Nobody's seen him.

Where could he have got to?

'He smashed up a table?' Ellie's jaw drops open when I tell her. 'I don't believe it!'

'And assaulted a customer!' I repeat.

'That's just not like Kai.'

'It's true. He must've been in a right state. And it's all my fault.'

'No it's not. It's mine. I was a right cow to him.'

We stare at each other miserably.

'What if he's done something stupid?' I whisper.

Ellie's face looks stricken. 'Like what?'

I shrug my shoulders, afraid to say.

She jumps into action. 'Look, I'm putting it on Facebook. Send me a recent photo of him from your phone.' She starts typing: 'HAS ANYONE SEEN KAI?'

'No, Ellie, don't post it.'

'Why not?'

'He'd hate it, that's why. You know what he's like. He's a very private person.'

She looks at me pityingly. 'So what? You want to find him, don't you?'

She's right. And Ellie's got more Facebook friends than anyone else in the world. I send her a photo and she publishes. Immediately her phone starts pinging and we start scanning through the responses.

No one has actually seen him since we did.

'At least it's getting out there,' says Ellie comfortingly. 'Someone will know where he's got to. He can't have vanished off the face of the earth.'

But he has. The responses keep coming. Lots of concern. No sightings.

My phone rings and I jump a mile. It's Mum. Her soap fest having come to an end, she's finally noticed that her daughter's missing. I tell her where I am and that actually, it's Kai who's disappeared, giving her the abridged version, of course. She's totally underwhelmed.

'For goodness sake Jen, he's a big boy now. Stop fussing around him like a mother hen!'

That stings but I ignore it. If I'd ignored Ellie when she said the same thing we wouldn't be in this predicament now. I know Kai. I need to find him and calm him down. Goodness knows what state he's in.

'I'm not coming home till I've found him,' I say stubbornly.

'And how do you propose to do that?' she says sarcastically. 'Send out a search party?'

Brilliant. Thanks Mum. That's exactly what I'm going to do. I switch her off and say to Ellie, 'Tell everyone to meet at the Beach Café.'

chapter 18
KAI

I'm fine. There's nothing to be afraid of.

I sit up and look around. The seal is still there. I can see quite a way now in the clear, silver moonlight. In the distance a red beam of light catches my eye as it flickers three times, on and off. Seconds later, it repeats.

A warning buoy. What's it for?

Dangerous rocks, probably. Or is it where the tides merge?

Why don't I know these things?

Most of the kids at school would because loads of them have dads, granddads and uncles who are lifeboat men, fishermen or coastguards. It's not fair. They've grown up with knowledge of the sea and know these waters like the backs of their hands.

Not me. The little I know, I've gleaned from Jen.

I don't even know who my dad is.

To be fair to Mum though, she taught me to swim. I can swim as well as anyone, thanks to her. She even used to take me night swimming when I was a kid.

I loved it.

I never learned to surf properly though. Not like the other kids who had dads and older brothers to teach them, or expensive surf lessons which we couldn't afford. I taught myself on an old board Mum bought at a car boot sale, by watching others and copying what I saw.

Now I can make out more lights scattered across the sea, not as bright as the buoy. Something's lit up, out on the horizon. A container ship, I guess. Or maybe a cruise ship, laden with passengers; the kind who sail all over the globe but never once dip their posh toes in the ocean. Closer in are individual lights. Smaller vessels. Fishing boats. Beam trawlers probably.

Plus one solitary light that seems nearer than the rest. Yet smaller. A lone owl, like Crabby.

My heart lifts. Maybe it *is* Crabby?

I turn around and try to measure how far I am from the shore. A couple of miles? Impossible to tell but I reckon the tide is still taking me out. Then I look out to sea and gauge the distance from me to that little bobbing light.

Closer. Loads closer. And I'd be going with the tide.

I chew the skin around my thumbnail like I always do when I've got a difficult decision to make and give myself a pep talk.

It's like this, mate. You can do nothing and wait to be rescued. Though, it doesn't look like a lot's happening in that quarter. Let's face it, you haven't exactly been missed.

Or you can do something about it, yourself.

I wince as a strip of skin tears free from my thumb, automatically licking the drops of blood that appear. They taste warm and metallic.

I lick my lips. They feel dry. I'm thirsty. How long is it since I ate or drank? If I stay out here much longer maybe I'll have to eat my own hand. Or drink my own pee! Isn't that what people have to do to survive?

And with that unsavoury thought to spur me on I lie down and start to paddle further out to sea in the direction of the small light, wincing as my thumb smarts in the salt water. My arms push through the inky sea and silvery bubbles appear around my board.

Phosphorescence. Sheer magic.

It's a good omen.

I keep my head down and plough my way steadily through the brine.

I'm going to make it to that boat.

I have to.

chapter 19
JEN

Ellie and I hot foot it down to Sandy Bay. By the time we get there loads of people have beaten us to it and there's quite a crowd milling about outside the café. All for Kai.

A figure detaches itself from the others. It's Jay.

'You alright?' he asks, giving me a hug. It's good to see him there, large and reassuring, with Macca behind him.

'Kai's gone missing. It's all my fault.'

'No, it's mine,' says Ellie.

'Actually, it's me who's responsible for him running off,' says Oliver, stepping forward. 'I sacked him.'

Jay holds his hands up. 'Whoa! Who cares whose fault it is? The important thing is, does anyone know where he could've got to?'

'Daft question, but has anyone tried his house?' someone asks.

'Yes, of course I have!' Then I remember, with a sinking heart, that I never called his mum back and the poor woman is under the illusion that I've spoken to him and he's OK. 'I'll try again.'

Don't panic, I tell myself. *Maybe he's home by now*. But as soon as she speaks, I know he's not.

'Jen? Is Kai alright?'

'It wasn't him. Someone found his phone on the beach,' I say in a rush and hear her sharp intake of breath. 'I don't know where he is.'

Jay takes the phone from my hand.

'Mrs Stevens?' His voice is calm, authoritative. 'This is Jay Curnow. Don't worry, we'll find him. I promise. We're looking for him now. Lots of us. I'll keep you updated.'

He ends the call, puts his hands on my shoulders and turns me round to face him.

'I'm sorry Jen, but I've got to ask you this. Is there any chance that Kai could have gone out on the water?'

My heart lurches. 'Oh God!' I look out at the night sky and the dark, boundless sea. 'I hope not. He knew we were heading over to the Pass. Do you think he might have tried to join us?'

Ellie's hand steals into mine. 'It's OK,' she says. 'Don't worry. Jay will sort it.'

118

chapter 20
KAI

It's easier paddling out to sea than trying to get back to shore. I'm no longer battling against the tide. I feel like I'm covering distance quickly but when I look up, I'm surprised to see that I've veered off course. I need to keep looking where I'm going.

When I stop for a breather I can feel the wind up again. Not surprising, I'm heading out into the vast Atlantic Ocean. Somewhere around here seven tides meet, so they say, and the currents are strong. At least going this way the breeze is behind me, helping me along. I look around for my seal but there's no sign of him.

Shit! He knows when he's gone too far. *What have I done?* Panic grabs me in its familiar choking fist.

Should I go back?

I'm going to drown!

Then I hear something. A deep, repetitive throbbing, like the beating of a pulse.

What is it? Some monster from the deep, come to swallow me up? A whale? The ocean?

No wonder the seal buggered off.

Calm down you nutter. You're going to reach the boat.

I lie down and continue propelling myself towards it and it's OK, I'm going with the current. And, with each sweep of an arm, I repeat those words like a mantra, in time to the beat:

Calm down, calm down. You're going to reach the boat.

Calm down, calm down. You're going to reach the boat.

When I stop for a rest, the noise is louder. It sounds like music.

I can see the silhouette of the vessel in the distance, low in the water with a tiny cabin and a winch at the front. It's a gillnetter – a one-man job, I'm guessing by the size of it – a net thrown over the back with holes big enough to let heads pass through, but not gills.

And so the fish get caught.

Sometimes other things get trapped in them, too. Like seabirds and seals and turtles. Jen hates them for that reason.

I need to get going again but I can't get that image out of my head. All I can think of is being tangled up in a gillnet. I close my eyes as the full horror of it washes over me.

Head in, shoulders trapped, arms and legs flailing.

Entangled in the mesh.

Lungs bursting, body snared.

Choking, choking.

Torn to shreds.

No escape.

My worst nightmare. Being trapped and unable to get away. I can't stand confrontation either. For me the two are linked together, I don't know why. I've been in loads of trouble at school over the years for storming out of class, though I haven't done that for a while.

Hmm. Today you stormed out of your job.

Don't remind me. Anyway, that's the least of my problems.

And then you did what you always do. You ran away.

I open my eyes and groan. For all the good it did me. I might as well be behind bars as out here under the stars. I'm still trapped. Only this time by my own stupidity.

I hear something new. A woman is singing. How bizarre is that? Is it the song of the mermaid calling me down to her ocean bed?

Don't be daft! You're not a kid anymore. There are no such things as mermaids.

Well somewhere, in the middle of this vast ocean, a woman is shrieking her head off. On and on and on she wails in some foreign language.

And then I get it. It's opera! And it's coming from the boat.

This is surreal. My black mood lifts and I find myself laughing in delight.

Don't share your taste in music, mate, but you know what? I'd love to hitch a ride back home with you.

Wait for me.

I'm on my way.

chapter 21
JEN

Jay is a trouper. He divides everyone up into groups led by the lifeguards and sends them off in different directions to search for Kai. Macca and Ben cover the beach from the Pass to the lighthouse, Danny does the town, while Jay and I set off on our own on the coastal path towards his house.

First we stop off at the lifeguard hut to pick up a torch.

Jay takes a sweeping look around inside.

'What are you doing?'

'Counting the surfboards.'

'Why?' Then the penny drops. 'You don't think Kai's taken one, do you? How could he? It was locked.'

'I don't think anything, Jen. I'm just doing my job. It's fine. They're all here.'

If this is meant to dispel my fears it's having the opposite effect. I've seen Jay the Lifeguard countless times but normally he's surrounded by admiring fans or charging up and down the shoreline on his quad bike.

Now Jay the Professional is in charge and it's making me nervous.

I think of what Ellie said.

'Jay will sort it.'

I wish I had her confidence.

chapter 22

KAI

Keep going, keep going. You're going to reach the boat.

Keep going, keep going. You're going to reach the boat.

I'm paddling like fury. When I next raise my head I can see the cabin lit up. The door is open and the music is belting out. Dimly, I can make out a shape standing on the deck.

'HELP!' I shout. 'HELP!'

But he's too far away to hear me over the noise of that bloody woman wailing. Just my luck to come across the one fisherman in Cornwall who's both opera mad and deaf.

What's he doing?

In answer, a pinprick of light flies in a perfect arc into the sea. He's been having a smoke.

He remains standing there for a while. I bet he's taking a pee. Then he moves towards the back of the boat and disappears from sight.

He must be checking his net.

'*H-E-E-E-L-P!*' I yell. 'I'M IN THE WATER!'

But all I get for my efforts is a mouthful of salty sea and a choking fit. I'm no match for an opera singer. I need to get closer.

I take a deep breath, get my head down and charge through the water, my arms whirling at the sides of my board like rotors. I am making the biggest effort of my life and I'm not going to stop till I get there. And the first thing I'm going to do is tell him to turn his bloody music down.

Only when I finally look up I've done it again. I've gone skew-whiff. My stronger right arm has made me swerve off to the left, further out to sea.

Keep your head up, you donkey, and watch where you're going!

I strike out again, this time keeping my eyes on the boat. My head is hurting, my arms are throbbing and my neck is aching. There is no sign of the owner and the music seems more contained. He's back inside the cabin with the door shut.

There's a new sound though. Crying and squawking. Seagulls are circling and wheeling above the boat.

Something else is different. It takes me a few seconds to realise what it is. The net has been pulled up out of the water. My heart drops.

He's emptied his catch into the bottom of the boat. Hence the seagulls. Now he's about to call it a day and head for home.

'Wait for me!' I shriek but silence mocks me and I swallow loads of salt water. There is no time to lose.

Coughing and spluttering I fork a path to the boat, determined to haul myself up on it by myself if he's too frigging deaf to hear me.

I'm nearly there. I can do it.

And then suddenly there's a thump and a roar and an outpouring of stinking, rotten diesel fumes that make me cough and gag as the engine kicks into life.

'Wait!' I wheeze, gasping for breath. 'Help me!'

Somehow, I lurch to my feet, and stand up on my board, rocking and swaying in the moonlight, my arms waving. And I take a huge breath and find my voice because I have to and shout and scream . . .

'HELP! HE-LP! *H-E-E-E-E-L-P!*'

But he can't hear me above the noise. No one could.

I overbalance and topple headfirst into the water. When I come up again I head straight for the boat but the leash jerks me back.

I have no choice. I rip it away from my ankle and swim for it. Banging up against the boat, I grab the rail to haul myself up out of the water. One hand. Two hands. HEAVE!

But I'm too late.

My screeches merge with the seagulls as the boat pulls away and I'm flung back into the sea.

chapter 23

MOONSHINE

The boy was tumbling through the ocean

    down

    down

    down

towards the bottom of the sea.

He thought he was alone, but he wasn't. Lots of creatures were watching him.

Like the garfish. A curious, bluey-green, eel-like fish with a beak, which studied him as he sank past. A red gurnard with bulging eyes swished his spiny legs at him. For in the strange world under the sea, some fish do have beaks like birds, while others have legs. Mackerel shot away like torpedoes in a flash of black stripes and silver bellies, and a shoal of whiting bolted after them, their mouths wide open in surprise.

Below him lay the ocean bed, where the wreck of the *April Flower* rested. It had been there so long it had come to life again. Covered in barnacles and kelp, it was home to flatfish such as sole and flounder, turbot and megrim, and countless other fish besides - some round, some disc-shaped, some long and slender - that live near the bottom of the sea.

Crabs scuttled sideways to make room for him while tube worms waved a welcome and sea urchins that look like hedgehogs budged up obligingly. Even the big old sea cucumber - which is an animal, not a vegetable - shifted over.

The boy opened his eyes and looked down, marvelling at the resplendent sea forest he could see below him with its beckoning seaweed, colourful coral, clumps of pretty pink sea anemones and vigorous, darting fish.

It was beautiful.

It was welcoming.

He wanted to stay here for ever.

chapter 24

JEN

Jay and I head out along the coast path towards Kai's. On the way we pass Jay's house; its white walls standing out against the dark night, the windows bright with light. Further back on the main road, music and laughter can be heard from the Miners' Tavern. These signs of normal life make me feel better. Kai can't be far away. We'll find him soon.

But as we continue along the path past the church and graveyard, spooky in the darkness, a tree reaches out to claw me with its long, skinny fingers and my mood plummets once more. We used to play here, Kai and me, when we were kids. I showed him the gravestones of people lost at sea over the years. There were so many of them.

'If they were lost at sea how could they get back here?' he asked me. But I didn't know.

An owl hoots and I nearly jump out of my skin.

The street lights disappear on the road above us and the track becomes more difficult to negotiate. I keep my eyes fixed to the ground and follow the beam of Jay's torch, trying my best not to trip up. The path meanders a lot and I can't see how far to step up or down. It's slippery too from the recent flash storm.

'Kai,' I mutter to myself like a prayer. 'Where are you?'

Suddenly I stumble, coming down heavily on my ankle, and pain shoots through me. It's not that bad, just unexpected, but I cry out.

'You OK?' asks Jay, and I am. But the darkness and the fear and the not knowing finally gets to me and I remain sprawled on the dank path, racked with deep, raw sobs. And Jay, bless him, is there for me instantly, with big brotherly hugs and pats on the back.

But it's Kai I want and no-one else and I don't know where he is. And those ugly, gut-wrenching sobs just won't stop coming from somewhere deep inside me until, in sheer desperation, I throw my head back and scream,

"KAI! COME BACK! I NEED YOU!"

chapter 25

KAI

I'm falling, falling, falling, into the deep ocean.

I'm sinking fast.

It's over. I know that now.

As my lungs are squeezed tight and my stomach contracts, the pressure is unbearable. My head feels like it's about to implode. I need to breathe!

Instead I open my eyes.

It's dark down here. But I'm aware of delicate fronds reaching out to me, darts and flashes, small arrows of movement and light, a clump of colour.

The deeper I go, weirdly, the less it hurts. My heartbeat is dropping rapidly and my chest feels less constrained. I can hear my pulse in my head, loud and slow . . . very slow . . . long gaps between each beat.

One . . .

Two . . .

Three . . .

Four . . .

THUD!

One . . .

Two . . .

Three . . .

Four . . .

THUD!

It's peaceful here. My head is nodding. I could sleep.

To die. To sleep.

I promised Jen. But it's different now. I'm OK with this.
With everything.

To sleep . . . perchance to dream . . .

'Kai! Where are you?'

My head jerks back.

It's her. She's upset.

Don't worry about me, Jen. It's too late.

'KAI!

COME BACK!

I NEED YOU!'

Her cry from the heart – urgent, desperate – breaks the
spell and I look up.

Above me is the surface. I can't see it but I know it's up
there somewhere.

Resisting the urge to take a deep breath I press my arms
close to my body and kick my legs,

kick,

kick,

kick,

up through the water towards a bright coin of light
where I finally burst through the skin of the sea
back to the world above.

chapter 26

MOONSHINE

You see, it was not time for the boy to rest there in the breathing, bustling graveyard of the ocean bed.

Not yet.

He could hear someone calling him.

Someone he loved.

So he followed the voice

up

up

up

through the rippling currents

and the mysterious moon-tide.

And love pulled him back

to the world above the sea.

chapter 27

KAI

Gasping and heaving, I draw long jagged, painful gulps of raw air into my lungs. Around me the world whizzes like a Catherine wheel as the moon spins and stars flash. My ears pop; my chest burns; I think my nose is bleeding.

I tread water until sea and sky stop merging into one and the moon stops revolving and stars stop flickering and the world slows down and is still.

The sea is glassy, flat and even as a mirror. There is not a breath of wind. The night is hushed.

Then I remember.

My board?

You idiot! You let it go!

I whip around, peering through the darkness and, lo and behold, there it is in a patch of moonlight, waiting for me like a faithful dog.

I swim towards it, haul myself up and tie my leash back on. Then I lie down in abeyance and wait.

I am here.
I'm alive.
It's enough.

chapter 28

JEN

By the time we get to Kai's house the clouds are breaking up and the moon is peeking out from behind them. Jay raps on the door and it opens almost instantaneously. The disappointment in his mum's face when she sees we're not Kai is like a knife in my heart.

We follow her in and I'm surprised how much nicer it is than I remember it. How long is it since I've been here? Ages. We hang out at Sandy Bay or in town nowadays.

The outside of the cottage looked much the same but inside the floorboards have been white-washed and her paintings and fabric work, all of them inspired by the sea, adorn the freshly painted walls. It's nothing like the depressing dump it used to be. It could be an art gallery.

She looks different, too. There's still a remnant of the old hippy in her long, now slightly greying hair, but the flowing skirts and patchy, washed-out tops have been replaced by tight jeans and a loose, stylish sweater. Her eyes are the same though: kind, watchful and a little bit lost.

'No news?' I ask and she shakes her head and tells us to sit down. I perch on the sofa, staring miserably at Kai's recent school photograph on the coffee table. A few more are scattered around. She's been looking at photos of him from a battered old biscuit tin, the kind you get at Christmas. I lean forward and pick one up.

It's Kai, smiling shyly at me through a curtain of long hair.

'Oh, this is how I first remember him,' I say in delight.

'Is that Kai?' remarks Jay. 'He looks like a little girl!'

What a crass thing to say in front of his mum. But it was true. If you didn't know him you'd have thought Kai was a girl back then. Everyone did. It was his hair. I used to tie it back for him so he wouldn't get teased.

The penny had eventually dropped that it made him stand out from the crowd and she'd allowed him to get it cut. He blended in then and looked just like any other kid in his school uniform.

My eye falls on another photo. A young couple with a baby. The baby is laughing on his mum's knee but even though she's smiling for the camera the smile doesn't quite reach her eyes. It's Kai's mum, much younger and, to be honest, a bit scruffy-looking. She looks exhausted.

So this is Kai as a baby. He's so cute. A big wide beam displaying his two bottom teeth. My eyes are drawn to the man beside them, holding the baby's hand, and my heart misses a beat. It could be Kai.

The man grins back at me from the picture. OK, it's an older version of Kai, mid-to-late twenties, perhaps, but it's him all right. Same nose, same thick dark hair, same crooked smile.

This has got to be his dad. He appears happy and proud in contrast to his mum who seems tired and strained, with dark circles beneath her eyes. He looks nice.

I stare nonplussed at him. Kai told me he never knew his dad, so I'm guessing he's never seen this picture. I glance around the room. On the shelves there are a few more framed school photos of Kai over the years, plus one of him and his mum. But none of him when he was little. Not like in our house where mine and my brother's baby photos are still permanently on display.

Jay clears his throat and stands up.

'Mrs Stevens, do you mind if I ask you a question?'

'Of course not. And please, call me Beth. Both of you.'

'Do you know if Kai's surfboard and wetsuit are here?'

'I guess so. He keeps them out the back.' She glances out of the window and her hand flies to her throat. 'Why? You don't think he went surfing, do you? But he'd be back by now, surely? It's so dark.'

'I'll just go and check,' says Jay and disappears outside.

Beth looks at me stricken. 'It's been dreadful out there tonight.'

I reach out my hand and she curls her fingers around it. We sit there together, holding hands tightly, not saying a word.

Waiting.

chapter 29
KAI

Sky and sea merge.
    I am part of it.
    Part of a much bigger whole.
    Resting.
    Resting.
    It's peaceful here.
    A gentle rocking.
    A rhythm.
    Beyond cold.
    Beyond fear.
    Beyond return.

chapter 30

JEN

Jay's bulk fills the doorway, his face serious. He's scaring me.

'They're still there,' he says and I jump up in relief.

'Phew! That's good. You had us worried for a minute.'

Beth sighs. 'Well, at least now we know that he's not out on the water on a night like this.'

But Jay still looks tense. 'We can't be sure of that. A lot of people are out searching the cliffs and the beach, but there's been no sign of him. I think it's time to look further afield.'

'What? You mean like see if he's got a bus or a train somewhere?' I turn to Beth. 'Where would he go?'

She's not listening to me. She's staring at Jay instead. 'You think he might have gone for a swim?' she says and my heart lurches.

'I don't know,' he says carefully. 'It was still light when he left the café. Do you think it's a possibility?'

'Well, yes, I suppose so. And he's a strong swimmer.'

'He knew we were going to the Pass,' I whisper. 'But that was hours ago.'

Beth stares out of the window at the night sky and bites her lip. 'It's pitch dark out there now.'

Jay makes up his mind. 'I'm sure he's fine. But I'm going to send out an alert. Just to be on the safe side.'

Everything happens very quickly after that.

Jay calls the coastguard. He's very crisp, factual and official. It's like he's talking about someone else, not Kai.

We listen as he tells him a fifteen-year-old boy is missing, following a disagreement with his girlfriend and an altercation at work at the Beach Café, Sandy Bay. He was last seen about seven p.m. in a state of distress. His phone has been found in the dunes at Sandy Bay.

Put like that it sounds really, really serious.

The coastguard must think so too. Ironically, Jay's pager goes off. They're launching the lifeboat at Sandy Bay.

'Got to go,' he says and this is the first time I see him in a flap. 'Oh shit! I'm never going to get there in time.'

'Take my car,' says Kai's mum and chucks the keys at him.

'I'm coming with you.' I jump to my feet.

'No! Wait here and phone the coastguard if he comes back,' he cries and disappears out of the door.

chapter 31
KAI

My mind is lucid again, as clear as the night. My feet and hands are numb. Even my skull is cold. My teeth feel like they're rattling about inside it.

Did you know that directly beneath the surface of the ocean on which I am drifting, there lies a world?

I'm not talking about a fishy world where marine life prospers. I'm talking about the lost world of Lyonesse. It lies off the tip of England between Cornwall and the Isles of Scilly. The Cornish pronounce it Lioness.

Alfred Lord Tennyson wrote about it many years ago as a place '. . . *where fragments of forgotten people dwell*'.

That's me. Sometimes I feel fragmented like a leaky, broken pot that's been stuck back together again any old how. And now, let's face it; it looks like I've already been forgotten.

I guess everyone is forgotten eventually.

Who would remember me? Mum. Jen. Oliver? Definitely Oliver, after today. Was it really only this evening that I smashed up a table at his restaurant? It can't be. It seems like a lifetime ago.

Maybe it's tomorrow already.

Who would recall me in years to come in a good way? A few mates, hopefully. One or two teachers, maybe? Mr Davis, English. And someone, kind and playful, who chucked a very young Kai in the air and laughed, and called him Kevin.

Where did that come from? I struggle hard to remember my mysterious playmate from years gone by but his face is blurred, like those fuzzy TV crime shots they show when they don't want bystanders to be identified.

The guy at the café today called me Kevin. But, somehow I know it's not him.

Anyway ... apparently, Lyonesse was swallowed up long, long ago on a single stormy night, so the story goes. Imagine the power of the ocean if it can drown a whole town. What chance have I got?

Strangely, I feel no fear. Instead I peer down into the still depths in search of that lost world, but it's too dark for me to spot the forgotten people going about their business in their 'sea-cold town.' That's a quote from another poet who wrote about it, Walter de la Mare.

Mare means sea. Walter of the Sea.

And there were others. Thomas Hardy. Sylvia Plath. Loads of people have been drawn to Lyonesse. Poets. Storytellers. Scholars. Mr Davis would be proud of me. I've read practically everything there is on the subject. So many variations of the same legend. Each story different; some hard to believe.

And yet, truly, I think there is something there. I know what storm-driven waves can do in this part of the world. I've seen the evidence myself.

Last winter they tore at our beaches uncovering, beneath the shifting sands, ancient forests, the ribs of an old longboat and remains of stone houses that led out beneath the sea. Each summer they pull unsuspecting holidaymakers to watery graves.

When you die is that the end?

The world goes on without you, sure enough.

But, can you go on without the world?

Maybe, soon, I'll find the answer.

I immerse my face in the sea, looking for all those broken, forgotten people.

chapter 32

LYONESSE

Soft dark shapes
    Hills
    Houses
    Tracks
    Sweeping down to a curved bay
    Hugged by rocks
    Calm and still.
    Shapes merge and melt
    In a gentle curving of sand and sea and civilisation
    Worked and tended by those long forgotten
    But still there
    Always there
    Though they cannot be seen.
    Yet sounds filter through
    Children's laughter
    Songs and sighs
    And phantom cries

The moaning of sea

And men

The chatter of women

And always the sound of bells

Calling me, calling me

Down from the shrinking world above.

Welcome to Lyonesse they toll.

Say farewell to those above and come rest with us now.

Rest with us here

In the deep lovely world beneath the sea.

chapter 33

JEN

I can't believe this is happening.

As soon as Jay leaves I moan, 'This is all my fault!' and collapse in a flood of tears. Beth takes me in her arms.

'Don't be silly.'

'You heard him. He went missing after a disagreement with his girlfriend!'

'Stop that now,' she says consolingly. 'Jay has to give them the background so they've got some idea of his state of mind, but no one's blaming anyone. And remember, he's expecting Kai to walk in any minute. It's just a precaution he's taking, that's all.'

I pull away from her. 'I'm going to look for him.'

'You don't know where he is, love.'

'Yes I do. Sandy Bay, of course. That's where he was last seen – and where his phone was found.'

'Jen, you don't know that for sure. Hold fire until we know more. Jay's got my car and you could break your neck out there tonight on those cliffs. I don't want you going missing too.'

She looks worried sick. 'He'll be fine,' she adds, her appearance belying her words. 'You know what he's like. He just needs some time to himself to cool off.'

She's far more scared than she's admitting. I can't leave her on her own so, bizarrely, I sit there doing nothing while she makes us sugary tea and the emergency services search for the most important person in the world to us both. I find myself rifling through the tin to find more photos of Kai before I knew him but there aren't any.

Just that one picture of the three of them. I pick it up again and study it carefully.

'Have you got any more photos of Kai as a baby?' I ask as she places the steaming tea in front of me. She looks surprised to see it there in my hand.

'No,' she says. She sits down and takes it from me, looking at it closely, and in all my life I have never seen anyone look so sad.

'He was a lovely baby,' I say carefully.

'Yes, he was,' she agrees. She picks up one of him when he was about seven on Porthzellan and passes it to me; then another of Kai, about ten, smiling shyly at the camera with a sports day medal around his neck. I remember that day vividly; he was so proud of himself.

Beth sighs heavily. 'He was a lovely boy too.'

'I know he was,' I say. We sit there examining photos of

him silently. And I think to myself, so long as we can keep focusing on him like this, he'll be OK.

Then I go cold as I realise what we're doing.

We're talking about him in the past tense.

As if he's dead.

She must think the same because suddenly she scoops up all the photos and crams them back into the tin. Then she rams the lid down on them.

As if, by doing so, she can keep him safe inside.

chapter 34
ELLIE

Jen's ringing me. I'm so nervous I nearly drop the phone.

'Any news?'

Her voice is low, almost a whisper. 'He wasn't at home. Where are you?'

'On the beach. Nearly everyone's back down here now. We've searched everywhere, Jen. There's no sign of him.'

'I know. They think he's in the water, Ellie. They're launching the lifeboat to look for him.'

'I can see them. Both of them are out there, the big one and the little one.'

'What's happening?'

'The big one's heading over towards the Pass.'

'They think he may have tried to swim over to meet us there. Oh, Ellie, why didn't I wait for him?' Her voice fades away into a moan.

My blood runs cold. The Pass is a hell of a way to swim. Plus it's really dangerous out there.

It was me who told him where we were going. *To the Pass. With guys who know how to have fun.* This is all down to me. I swallow hard.

'Jen, speak up babe. I can't hear you properly.'

'I don't want Kai's mum to hear me. Ellie, he's been gone for ages.'

She doesn't sound like Jen. She sounds scared stiff. Desperate.

'Can you get over here?'

'No, I can't leave his mum.'

'D'you want me to come to you?'

'Yes . . . No. It's better if you stay where you are. I need to know what's going on.'

'Is Jay there with you?'

'No. He's on the lifeboat, I think.'

'That's good. They'll find him, Jen. Don't worry.'

'But Ellie . . . what if it's too late?' she whimpers. 'What if he's already drowned?'

Poor Jen. She's normally the grown-up in our friendship. Now, for the first time ever, she needs me to be strong.

'He'll be fine, Jen,' I say firmly with a conviction I don't really feel. 'Jay will bring him back.'

chapter 35
JEN

The worst thing in the world is waiting. Sitting doing nothing, while everybody else is out there doing something. I feel like I've been stuck here for ever.

At last the telephone rings and Beth jumps up to answer it. 'Yes,' she says, and 'Yes,' again and I watch the colour draining from her face. 'Yes, that's right,' she says, her voice now no more than a whisper. Then she hangs up and sits down heavily as if her legs won't support her anymore.

It's bad news.

'Who is it? Have they found him?' But I'm hunched over with my fingers in my ears so I can't hear the answer because the truth is, I'm terrified and I don't want to know. Don't tell me.

'That was Cliff Rescue. No, they haven't found him.' I take my hands away, not sure whether I should be pleased or upset. 'But they've found his clothes.'

'What?' *How could they find his clothes and not him?* 'Where?'

'Near the lighthouse. Rolled up and stuffed in a hedge. They wanted me to identify them. They're his all right.'

'What does that mean? Why would he take his clothes off?' I'm struggling to make sense of this. 'So, he's gone for a swim after all? That's good isn't it?' I stare at her hopefully. 'He's a strong swimmer. You said so yourself.'

She sits there hugging herself tight, looking like her soul's been ripped out. Suddenly, long, scraping, ugly sobs rack her body, filling the room with their haunted lament. And then I get it.

Clothes rolled up and stuffed in a hedge. By the lighthouse.

She doesn't think that he's gone for a swim at all.

She thinks he's thrown himself off the rocks.

She thinks he's taken his own life.

chapter 36
KAI

I raise my face from the sea, gasping for breath, and shake my hair free of water.

Careful, Kai! Leave Lyonesse alone. Your mind is playing tricks on you. Next you'll be chasing a mermaid down to her watery boudoir. I think Jen might have something to say about that.

I sit up and look around.

Moonlight. Starlight. Calm. Stillness.

Huge.

It hits me how small I am. Nothing, but a tiny spot on a glorious fish-eye landscape of sea and sky, which have softened and merged into one.

But, weirdly, this sense of my own insignificance in no way diminishes me. Instead fear has dropped away like the setting sun and wonder has taken its place, expanding like a flower, reaching out to light and space.

I hear the sea murmuring below me and feel the gentle swell chaffing at my board.

I slip my arms into its sharp, silken cold.

I breathe in its salty, fishy smell and taste it on my dry, chapped lips.

I lift my face and watch, spellbound, as a cloud trails wispy fronds across the face of the moon.

I have never felt so present in my life.

I AM HERE.

I AM THIS MOMENT.

I AM KAI.

chapter 37

JEN

The lifeboats have searched the area around the lighthouse and now they are making their way slowly back to Sandy Bay. I'm watching them from the Point where I'm standing with my arm around Beth, the beams on their masts bright signals in the night, their powerful spotlights sweeping over the water.

I can't believe this is happening.

They found no sign of Kai. Neither did the rescue team who scoured the cliffs above, flashing their torches down the many mine shafts, capped but still dangerous, that puncture this land. Beth and I searched too, shouting, 'Kai? Kai! Where are you?' but he didn't answer.

Now the lifeboats are retracing the swim he might have taken back towards the bay and if they don't find him on the way they will check the rocks and pools of the shoreline where he could be stranded.

The swim he *might* have taken . . . where he *could* be stranded. No one knows what's happened to him, that's the trouble, it's all guesswork. He could be anywhere, on land or sea.

'You know what?' says Beth quietly. 'I can't help feeling if he was going for a swim he'd have gone off Porthzellan.'

She's remembering the times she spent there on the beach with him when they first came down to Cornwall, before he'd started school. It was a special place for them then. But he's moved on from those days. It's Sandy Bay we hang out at now.

'Hmm, maybe.' I stare out at the vast expanse of ocean and shiver. It's cold tonight.

It will be even colder in the water.

Actually, temperature-wise it will be the same, or even higher. The sea temperature is still relatively warm at this time of year: about ten degrees. You'd be fine if you were walking about in that. But the trouble is the human body cools about twenty-five times faster in cold water than in the same air temperature and hypothermia soon sets in.

Listen to me, I sound like a text book. I learnt all this at Junior Life-Saving Club on summer weekends as a kid. It was fun. We used to have competitions. I won most of them. I know that you can't survive in the water for long. If you fall in, assuming you survive the cold shock immersion and don't have a heart attack, you've got about an hour, max. If you're lucky.

It's almost eleven p.m.

Kai has been missing for nearly four hours.

chapter 38
KAI

I am lying on my back, moonbathing. Oddly, I don't feel so cold anymore. My mind is open, like a wound.

I have no idea how far I've drifted out. But strange to say, it no longer bothers me.

The sea is singing to me softly. A lullaby.

When I was little my mother used to sing to me to send me to sleep. My favourite song was 'Que Sera, Sera.' That's Spanish for 'whatever will be, will be.' The chorus went like this:

Que sera, sera,
Whatever will be, will be,
The future's not ours to see,
Que sera, sera.

A strange choice but I loved it. Because the truth was, when I was a kid, I never had a clue what the next day would bring. But you know what? Always, through that wild time, there was that song of my mother's to lull me to sleep. And strangely, I found it comforting because, even though I didn't know what my future held, it implied it would be good.

I have no idea what will happen to me now.

Que Sera.

Suddenly memories start seeping from my mind like a septic sore.

Early morning exits before anyone else was awake.

A bus to somewhere new.

And so it would begin all over again.

New bloke.

New place to bed down.

Dark, smoky nights and wild, raucous laughter that woke me from my dreams.

The sweet smell of cider and wine, cigarettes and something else.

New story.

But the next day, or the day after, or the day after that we'd move on again. To a different version of the same story.

Same old.

As I lie on my back under the age-old stars, looking back at the past and listening to the sound of the sea lapping around me, I become that small child again.

And remember things I never knew I'd forgotten.

chapter 39
KAI'S STORY

One man we stay with for a while and it's nice. He's called Darren and he makes Mum laugh. He likes me too. He says we're best mates and spoils me rotten. He buys me chips and coke and we watch movies together on his laptop.

One day we're in the middle of this movie which has got lots of fighting and shooting in it and Mum comes in and switches it off. Darren shouts at her so I do too but secretly I'm glad because it's scary. He switches it back on and she switches it back off and it's funny, the laptop going on and off like that, it makes me laugh.

But then it won't work anymore and Darren gets really cross and there's BIG SHOUTING and BLOOD and I run away and hide under the bed. And the next day Mum's got a thick lip and a swollen cheek and Darren's sorry but it's not his fault because she shouldn't have touched his laptop. And then he takes us out for milkshakes and everything's alright again.

After that Mum's really careful and tries not to do things wrong – only sometimes she doesn't quite manage it and then Darren's cross again and I run away and hide.

'It's not Darren's fault,' Mum explains, giving me a cuddle in bed one morning. 'He's got a short fuse.'

She looks like she's winking at me because one eye won't open properly but it doesn't make me feel like laughing. The night before I'd woken up to shouting and sobbing again and I'd curled up into a tight ball under the blanket until it stopped. Then I must have fallen back to sleep.

I feel bad about it now, looking at her winky-wonky eye.

'Like a firework?'

'Exactly like a firework, clever boy,' she laughs. 'Light his fuse and you'd better stand back because he goes POP!'

I reach out and touch her swollen eyelid gently, tracing the different colours. Red and purple and blue, like roman candles. Black and yellow from last week's explosion.

Mum winces. She sits up on her elbow and stares down at me with her good eye.

'Listen, Kai,' she says, her voice serious. 'Promise me you'll be a good boy and keep out of Darren's way.'

'I promise.' I catch a single teardrop oozing from the corner of her shut eye on the tip of my finger and lick it. It tastes of the sea. 'Tell me the story of the mermaid again.'

So she does. It's one of my favourites. When Mum was little like me she'd gone to Cornwall on holiday and she

162

said there were mermaids there. When she finished the story I say, 'Can you take me to Cornwall one day to look for mermaids?' and she says she will.

One night soon after, Darren is being giddy and making us laugh. Then other people turn up with bottles of beer and wine and other stuff and it's like a party. Mum's drinking wine out of a bottle and laughing a lot and she looks really pretty.

'Time for bed Kai, I'll be there in a minute,' she says, but she doesn't come.

I must've fallen asleep because I wake up and someone is shrieking and it sounds like the party's still going on but then I can tell it's not shrieking-laughing, it's shrieking-crying and it's Mum, so I jump out of bed and go and see.

Everyone's gone except for Mum and Darren. Mum is rolled up on the floor in a tight ball with her head in her hands, like me in bed when I want to keep bad things out, but Darren isn't helping her up. Instead he's standing over her, shouting horrible names at her, and I'm scared.

She lifts her head and screams, 'Leave me alone!' and tries to crawl away. But Darren does something really bad. He stamps down hard on her leg and she can't move. She's like that mouse I once saw stuck in a trap – only she's not squeaking, she's howling like a dog, like it really hurts.

Then he grabs her by the hair and pulls her head back so his face is right up next to hers. 'You're going nowhere,' he bawls and his spit is on her and I don't like it. I can't breathe. I want my mum. And then he slaps her face hard.

'NO!' I shout, and I jump on his back and punch and kick him.

He picks me off and hurls me across the room and I can feel myself sliding down the wall and then it all goes black.

When I open my eyes again everything is topsy-turvy. Darren is on the floor and Mum is standing over him only he's not curled up tight, he's sprawled out fast asleep. His laptop is on the floor and it's got blood on it.

Mum turns around and stares at me with big, scared eyes and I know what she's thinking. Darren is going to be really cross when he wakes up.

'Come on, Mum,' I say, tugging at her. 'Let's go.'

So we grab our stuff and I take her by the hand and lead her down the stairs and into the night, even though she's the grown-up and I'm four-and-a-quarter.

We walk through the dark streets till we come to a big railway station. A train is waiting to pull out and it's going to Penzance.

'Where's that?' I ask.

'Cornwall,' says Mum.

'Can we go there?'

'Why not?'

So we go to Cornwall.

To look for mermaids.

164

chapter 40
JEN

I bite my lip to stop myself crying out loud and tell myself fiercely to stop tormenting myself. Kai didn't fall in. Think about it logically. He took his clothes off and went in deliberately, which means that he went for a swim. It makes sense. You wouldn't take your clothes off to chuck yourself over a cliff. Would you?

Kai would never end his life intentionally. He's a survivor. He wouldn't do it to me and he definitely wouldn't do it to his mum. Look how he took care of her when he was little, like he was the grown-up and she was the kid.

No, he's far more likely to have set off swimming and then found he'd bitten off more than he could chew. We don't know what time he started . . . there was that storm! Perhaps he got caught in a rip current!

I have to stop here to push down the new wave of terror that threatens to engulf me. *Deep breaths. Think it through.*

OK, worst-case scenario: he got caught in a rip. Well, Kai's a bloody good swimmer; he'd have known what to do. He would've swum off course to get out of it and so now he'll be further down the coast somewhere, trying to get back.

Or maybe he's stuck on a rock or at the bottom of a cliff, freezing cold and waiting to be rescued.

Let's face it, he could be anywhere!

I focus on the sea and sky and breathe in, out, in, out, slowly and deeply, trying to calm myself down. The clouds are breaking up. Suddenly the sky splits open to reveal a full moon that bathes the ocean in liquid luminescence.

My heart stops racing and I watch as a light wind chases shadows across the water and suddenly I know, without a doubt.

Kai – my best friend, the love of my life – you're out there somewhere. I know you are.

Looking for mermaids.

chapter 41
KAI

It's strange how that childhood episode has come back to me, out here, clear as day. It's like being alone on the ocean has stripped away the protective veneer that has hidden me from my past and revealed layers of consciousness that I never knew were there.

I know it's not my imagination playing tricks on me though. It's the truth.

Mum is a great mum. I can't begin to think what she's going through now. But she's had her moments, even since we washed up in Cornwall.

The trouble was she just wanted to hide herself from the world. She got herself a job cleaning caravans and we got by, though every so often when things went wrong she'd take refuge in the bottle, boozing herself to oblivion, forgetting that she had a small boy to feed, wash and get to school.

In those early years, Jen saw her at her worst a number of times. And when I begged her not to tell in case my mum got into trouble, she didn't because we were best friends. Instead she took me under her wing, inviting me home for tea, bossing me into shape. And lucky for me – or not, depending on which way you look at it – people tend to live and let live around here. I think her parents probably guessed my home life was pretty crap but thought my mum was doing her best.

And Mum did get better. *Eventually.* She sorted herself out, got off the booze and now she makes a tidy living making jewellery and artefacts inspired by the sea that are popular with locals and tourists alike. They're really good. She won't take it to the next level though, even though people are always saying she should. No internet presence for her.

'We make enough to live on,' she'd say. 'Why do we need more?'

I think it's because she doesn't like drawing attention to herself. She's such a private person: she'd hate the limelight.

She's never told me a thing about my dad. I don't even know what his name is.

Maybe it's just as well. He's probably just another Darren. He could even be Darren! I don't want to be like him. The one thing that scares me nowadays is my temper. I must've inherited it from my father, whoever he is.

People think I'm mild and easy-going but I'm not. Sometimes, especially if someone upsets me, I feel anger bubbling away inside and I'm terrified one day it will boil over and seriously hurt someone, just like Darren hurt

Mum. Look what happened earlier on at the Beach Café for goodness sake. Chucking a table over and threatening some random bloke just because he mixed me up with someone else. And all the time it was Oliver's and Macca's heads I wanted to punch in.

And so I ran away. Like I always do.

Just like Mum.

Too much thinking, Kai.

Switch your mind off.

Get back to the present.

chapter 42

JEN

I tell Beth I'm going to head back to Sandy Bay to see what's going on over there and hitch a lift from one of the Cliff Rescue people. On the way we pass a car speeding in the other direction. Someone's in a hurry. I call Mum en route to let her know where I am. She's mortified now she knows how serious the situation is.

I can't believe the scene when I get there. Literally hundreds of people with torches are combing the beach and shoreline, with plenty more on the cliffs. Across the bay the lifeboats are moving to and fro in combo, the inshore exploring rocks and pools while the big one is sweeping the water further out with its huge spotlight. Out there, the *dub dub dub* of a helicopter echoes eerily, its beam lighting up the bay. It's like a scene from a movie.

Unreal.

Ben's at the hut. He's getting the defibrillator ready. That's when it hits me. I stare at him, numb with fear.

'You're expecting to find him dead.'

'No! No way! We're not giving up on him, Jen,' he says quickly. Too quickly. 'Danny's out on his board now, looking for him.'

'And Macca?'

'He's been out there too. Someone's just run him home to fetch his own board.'

'What for?'

'He wanted to have a scout around in the sea by the lighthouse.'

That must have been them in the speeding car. I reflect on the significance of his words.

'You heard Kai's clothes have been found there, then?'

'Yeah. Jay let us know there was no sign of anyone in the water and they've resumed the search over here instead. But you know Macca – he wanted to make doubly sure.'

I nod. These guys always go the extra mile. My eyes fall on the row of boards. 'Can I take one out to look for him?'

Ben shakes his head regretfully. 'You know I can't allow you to do that.'

I think about just grabbing one anyway and rushing off into the water with it but I know that would be stupid. Instead I watch the lifeboats tearing back and forth and wail in frustration, 'They're just going over and over the same ground. What's the point of that?'

Ben looks at me pityingly. 'They know what they're doing, Jen.'

171

'But what if he's swum further out? Why don't you do something?'

I run off down the beach straight into the sea. The storm has disturbed a load of seaweed and its slippery strands swirl around my legs, clutching at me like slimy fingers. I stumble about in the shallows, tears forming. My wet clothes are clinging to me uncomfortably and it's cold, so cold. What chance has Kai got in the sea tonight?

Kai. I try to summon him up, the look, the sound, the feel of him, but he's not there. Instead the smell of rotting seaweed consumes me and all I can think of is death and decay.

I want to be out there with him.

'Jen!' Someone is calling me and for a second I think it's him and my heart leaps but it comes again from behind me, louder and more urgent this time. 'JEN! What do you think you're doing?'

Ellie and Ben are by my side, pulling me back on to the sand.

'Macca's been in touch,' says Ben.

This time my heart misses a beat. 'Has he found him?'

'No. But his board's gone. And his wetsuit. They've disappeared from the shed.'

'So?' This doesn't seem that important on the scale of things.

'We think Kai may have taken them,' explains Ben. 'If so, he could be much further out than we thought.'

He calls the coastguard and they widen the search. We watch from the shore as the lifeboats and helicopter respond and move further out to sea.

172

'We're getting there, Jen,' says Ben. 'We'll find him, don't worry.'

Ellie hugs me tight. 'Won't be long now,' she says and I allow myself a tiny glimmer of hope.

But hours later, we're still watching and they're still searching.

chapter 43
KAI

Time passes.

The moon crosses the sky.

The sea is calm and, curiously, so am I.

I have stopped beating myself up.

I have let go.

It wasn't hard. The sea has taken me over.

I have become part of it.

My breathing has slowed down.

I'm breathing with the ocean.

Details catch my eye. I focus on each one in turn.

A white curl of wave.

A dark swirl of water.

A ribbon of weed.

A sliver of moonlight.

A fish nibbles at my toe and a star falls from the sky.

The universe is huge and I am a speck in an ocean.

Time has no meaning anymore.

I can't feel the cold.

I am at peace.

I am one.

chapter 44

MOONSHINE

The boy was sailing on the ocean.

He had set out from one world and discovered another,

Pulled by the moon and the tides and the winds.

For as he moved away from the fret and fuss of stormy waters

To the blue-black hush of a calm sea,

A change came upon him.

The gentle waves washed away the cares that weighed him down.

The bright stars chased away the fears that made him run away,

And acceptance enfolded him in her warm, soft blanket.

And though he did not forget those he loved,

For never would he forget the woman or the girl,

He let go of all thoughts of getting back to that old world

And was free at last.

For he knew that whatever happened, it would be fine.

So a stillness settled on him

And time ceased to be.

chapter 45

JEN

Beth was right all along. Why didn't I listen to her?

Because I thought I knew best. As usual.

I don't answer my phone when I see it's Mum calling me. I've already made up my mind; I'm not going home till they've found him. Then the ping sounds for a text message and I have to take a peep in case it's Kai but it's her again.

I can see the first few words on the home screen:

I think Kai may be . . .

I open it quickly

. . . in the sea off Pz. Call me.

I ring back, my hands shaking, and she picks up straightaway.

'Your dad's just got home from a lock-in at the pub,' she says in a rush. 'He says Crabby was in earlier mouthing off about how he'd had to warn some daft lad with a surfboard heading over towards Porthzellan that a storm was brewing. Your dad didn't think anything of it at the time but now we're wondering. Jen, do you think it might have been Kai?'

'Ben!' I yell and then everything kicks off.

By the time we get to Porthzellan Cove both boats have already made it across from Sandy Bay and are searching close to shore and around the rocks. I phoned Beth on the way and she's down here already, a lonely silhouette on the water's edge.

'What are they doing?' I shout in frustration as I reach her side. 'They're looking in the wrong place. He's on a bloody surfboard. He could be miles out by now.'

But Beth doesn't answer.

So I turn to Ben who's driven me and Ellie here but he just stares at me and I say, 'What?'

But again there's no reply. It's like they're both frozen solid.

'*WHAAAAT*?' I scream, because I don't get it and nobody will tell me what's going on.

And then he says, his voice all quiet and flat so I know it's bad, 'We don't know this, Jen, but he could've fallen off his board and been washed back in. They've got to check.'

And then I get it.

They're searching for his body.

chapter 46

KAI

drifting, breathing,

    drifting, breathing . . . sky in sea, sea in me,

        no more lines, shapes and shadows . . .

           softening, shuffling,

                world is shrinking . . .

                    sshh . . . sshh . . . sshh . . .

                        . . . gone

chapter 47

JEN

Please God, he's still out there, somewhere, alive.

Beth and I are standing here together on Porthzellan Cove, clinging tightly to each other, like if we let go we'll fall down. I'm shaking, beside myself with cold and fear. The lifeboats are miles out now, systematically going back and forth across the sea, and we never take our eyes off them.

It feels like we've been here a lifetime.

Every so often I peer at them through Ben's binoculars and I can see as well as the spotlights at the front of the big lifeboat, someone is sweeping the sea to the sides with another bright light, searching the water. I wonder if it's Jay. They're much further out now than they were at Sandy Bay. That's because they've estimated how far the current might have taken him though Ben says they can't be precise because they don't know exactly what time he went in the water.

One thing is for sure though. If I'd listened to Beth when she said he'd make for Porthzellan Cove, we'd have had a better chance of finding him alive. We've lost valuable time and I blame myself for that.

The helicopter is out there too. In the distance I can hear the low thrum of its engine rather than the persistent *tch tch tch* of its blades if it was directly overhead. Its light is powerful but I'm not fooled. The ocean is so vast it's like looking for a needle in a haystack. When it flew over us I got excited because I could see something in the water but it just turned out to be that old seal that's made his home here for years.

Then I remember how Kai once told me how he loved that same seal as a kid because it made him feel safe. And even though he never said safe from what, I find myself thinking . . . hoping . . . praying . . . that it's a good omen.

Hundreds of people have made their way over from Sandy Bay and are out here scouring the beach and the cliffs, just in case. Mum and Dad, friends and neighbours have arrived, laden with flasks of tea and coffee for everyone. Bizarrely, I find myself thinking, if you didn't know better this could be a fun day out. Only it's dark, the atmosphere's tense, faces are sombre, voices are mute and it's cold – bitterly cold – now the wind has whipped up again.

I can't take a hot drink myself. It seems wrong now I know Kai is out there all alone with nothing to sustain him. Though I do appreciate the kindness. I look around and can't believe my eyes. So many people have come to help, their torches bright beams of hope in the darkness. Even old Crabby has turned up. I expect, like me, he's upset that he didn't do more.

I am surrounded by love. But the person I love most of all isn't here.

'What are they doing?' asks Ellie, bringing my attention back to the sea. The big lifeboat has come to a halt.

'Oh my God, they've found him!' I snatch the binoculars from Ben's neck, practically strangling him in the process.

But there's no one to be seen on board or in the water.

'Where have they got to?' I ask, bewildered, and Ben grabs back the binoculars and peers through them.

'They've gone inside the wheelhouse.'

'Why?' Terror grabs me by the throat. 'They're not coming back, are they? They haven't given up?'

'No, they wouldn't do that. I'm guessing they're taking a break.'

'Taking a break?' I stare at him, aghast. 'Are you kidding? Kai is out there somewhere on that freezing water. He could die of hypothermia while they're taking a bloody break!'

'It's OK, Jen, calm down. Stack Davey, the coxswain, knows what he's doing. They're cold too and now they'll be warming up and working out their next move at the same time. If it's humanly possible those guys will bring him back.'

I want to believe him. But it's the words, *IF.* And, *HUMANLY.* Neither of them exactly inspire confidence.

Beth must think so too because she sighs deeply. 'Maybe it's divine intervention we need here.'

I look at her, surprised. 'Do you believe in God?'

She bites her lip. 'I didn't think so. But all I know is I haven't stopped praying since my son went missing.'

183

'Me too.'

A cough behind us. It's Crabby.

'Scuse me, Missus,' he says. 'That puts me in mind of an old story.' And he clears his throat and starts to tell it, even though nobody asks him to.

'Once upon a time there was a great flood. A good and faithful servant climbed up to the highest point of the land. But still the waters rose up around him.'

I catch Ellie's eye. 'This is all we need right now,' she mutters, a bit too loud. 'He's a right weirdo.' But Crabby carries on regardless.

'At last he sees a fishing boat coming to his rescue.

"*No thank you*," says the servant. "*God will save me.*" So the boat left.'

I shake my head. Ellie's right. With his white beard and gruff loud voice, Crabby could be one of those crazy old preacher guys from years ago. And there's no stopping him.

'Then a yacht comes by and offers help.

"*No thank you*," says the servant, "*God will save me*," and the yacht sails away.

'Finally a cruise ship appears and lets down a lifeboat.

"*No thank you*," says the servant, "*God will save me*," and the cruise ship departed.'

'Very helpful,' remarks Ben drily. But still Crabby continues.

'So then the waters rose up and covered the highest point of the land and the servant drowned.'

184

We all exchange horrified looks.

'Well, thanks for that, Crabby,' says Ellie, sarcastically. 'Very comforting.'

'Hold your horses,' he says. 'I ain't finished yet. The good and faithful servant goes up to Heaven and meets God. "*Why didn't you save me, God?*" he asks.

"*I blooming well tried to,*" says God, "*I sent you a fishing boat, a yacht and a cruise ship. But you turned them all away.*"'

Crabby points to the lifeboats and the helicopter. 'That's your divine intervention out there, doing their job. If anyone can save him it's those guys.'

I follow his gaze. *OK, I get it. Thanks, Crabby.*

Though, even as I wonder what Kai would have to say about that little story I can't help noticing that, in the short time it's been idle, the lifeboat has drifted away from the main search area.

And I feel like throwing my head back and screaming at the heavens above, so much for your divine intervention, mate.

But then the moon peeks out from behind a cloud and a pathway of silvery light opens up from the big lifeboat to where Beth and I are standing. And, despite everything, a tiny spark of hope ignites and flickers into life inside me.

You know what, Kai? This thing is bigger than you and me.

It's time to hand over to the experts.

PART
THREE

chapter 1

JAY

When my pager went off I jumped straight into Beth's car and drove hell for leather to Sandy Bay. I tore into the lifeboat station but I was too late. Stack Davey, coxswain of the all-weather lifeboat, the *Lucy Ellen*, and the smaller inshore lifeboat, the *James Paddy Mick*, had already picked his crew.

Inside the station all I can see is a heaving mass of yellow waterproof clothing and red lifejackets. It looks like Stack's decided to send out both boats because some of the guys are getting into the body suits and helmets needed for the more exposed conditions of the smaller vessel.

'Can I come?' I plead. 'It's Kai Stevens who's missing. My cousin's boyfriend.'

I can tell in an instant the answer's no.

Too close, too emotional, too wet behind the ears.

Before he can open his mouth I add quickly, 'I know this area like the back of my hand, you know I do. And I know

189

Kai. I think he's gone in by the dunes opposite the Beach Café. I reckon he could have tried to swim to the Pass.'

Stack, a man of few words, stares at me for a brief second then says tersely, 'Get kitted up, quick. All-weather.'

I dive into my mustos, the yellow dungarees all crewmen wear, before he can change his mind. Then I tug on my boots and jacket, swallowing a pang of pride as I see my own name emblazoned on it, and grab a red lifejacket. Thank God for my local knowledge. That's why Stack took me on in the first place, that and the fact I'm a lifeguard and my dad had served on the lifeboat alongside him, until he damaged his back on a shout and had to give up.

In principle, you can be a lifeboat volunteer from the age of seventeen. I applied on my seventeenth birthday. It was all I ever wanted to be. But Stack, the coxswain, wasn't a big fan of taking on youngsters because he thought they were unreliable, as in too fond of the beer. He made an exception in my case, though he put me through a vigorous training programme to make sure I was up to it.

Medical. Fitness. Basic exercises. Introduction to lifeboat layout, engine room, lifejackets. After that, three months of Sunday mornings spent learning all about rope work and flares and launching and berthing and towing and anchoring and a million other things. Then he assessed me and it was like Stack was looking for any old excuse to fail me but I did it, I passed, and the day I got my very own pager was the proudest day of my life.

I'll never let him down.

I follow the others onto the *Lucy Ellen*. The engine's already started and the navigational systems are up and running. We need to get a move on. Kai's been out there for ages.

'Righto,' shouts Stack. 'Let go the ropes.' And I'm all fingers and thumbs because I'm rushing, and I know he's noticed because he never misses a trick.

He briefs us as we set off, what we're doing, where we're going, who we're looking for and the dangers of the bay but I know all this already. We start close to shore, which is what we always do if we're looking for a lone swimmer. Even if they've been dragged out to sea, they may have been washed back in.

As we head in the direction of the Pass the full horror of it all suddenly overwhelms me and my stomach heaves. This isn't any old shout. It's not some random holidaymaker we're looking for who's underestimated the power of the sea and needs a hand getting back to dry land. It's Kai, my little cousin's best mate and more than that by the look of it, and he's been missing for hours. It's his dead body we might be finding amongst these rocks.

I can feel myself losing it. *Why are we wasting valuable time this close to shore? He could be miles out to sea, exhausted and struggling to get back in. But where? If the bay is big, the ocean is bloody enormous. He could be anywhere!*

'Calm down, boy,' says a quiet voice. 'You know the drill. Treat this as an exercise.'

Stack is beside me, solid and unflappable. His presence dampens down the panic and I take a few deep breaths, pull myself together and transition into automatic mode.

'Got a job for you,' he says and hands me a spotlight. 'Midship,' he orders and climbs back up on the bridge, leaving me to get on with it.

I know what I have to do. Man this powerful light, sweeping it over the water to look for Kai.

I won't mess up. I can do this.

There's nothing to the east of Sandy Bay so we head west towards the lighthouse. It crosses my mind that Kai might have gone in for a swim off Porthzellan, a little cove the other side of the lighthouse and much closer to home for him. But the little information we have tells me there's nothing to suggest that: he hadn't been home after work or his mother would've seen him; the last sighting of him was at Sandy Bay; plus, his phone had been found there in the dunes.

No clothes to suggest he'd gone in for a swim, though. Jen was pretty upset. They'd obviously had a barney. Please God he hasn't done something stupid like throw himself off the cliff. *Would Kai do that?* I'm not sure what he's capable of. He's a bit of a loner. Apart from Jen, I don't think anyone really knows what goes on inside his head.

Concentrate. Cloud keeps blocking out the moon and stars so the spotlights are absolutely necessary. Gradually we move further out, about three-hundred metres at a time, and keep criss-crossing the bay from east to west, from the

Pass to the lighthouse and back again, leaving the inshore to double-check the shallows. All the time I'm sweeping the sea with my spotlight.

And then I see it.

A flash of white on the surface of the water.

Gone.

Then there it is again.

chapter 2

JAY

It's a flipping seagull.

False alarm. Thankfully, Stack was OK with it. 'Better to call out than be afraid of getting it wrong,' he says.

'Do you want a break?' he adds but I shake my head.

'I'm fine.'

He stands and watches me for a while then, satisfied, goes back into the wheelhouse.

A rescue helicopter joins us and circles the bay. Its huge light and the sound of its blades when it passes directly overhead, a distinctive, powerful, familiar throb – *tch tch tch tch* – fills me with reassurance. And I hope and pray that somewhere out there it will pass over Kai, and he will hear it too and know that help is on its way.

Then we get a call. Kai's clothes have been found in a hedge by the lighthouse.

Immediately we change tack and head over to search the rocks around the area near the lighthouse, while the inshore lifeboat scours the western shoreline. The helicopter follows us. It's choppy over here, the northerly wind, unusual for these parts, whipping up white horses in the sea. Along with more floating seabirds, they make my heart leap with false hope. But there's no sign of Kai.

At last Stack calls a halt.

'What do you think?' he asks me.

I hesitate, afraid of giving the wrong information.

'I reckon he was making for home then changed his mind and went in the sea.' I lick my lips nervously. 'His head was all over the place. He could have decided to swim back to Sandy Bay to make it up with Jen. Or he may have tried to swim even further, to the Pass where the rest of us were hanging out, like he had something to prove? I don't know. I'm guessing.'

Stack takes a deep breath and exhales. 'As good a guess as any. Either way, let's head back that way.'

So that's what we do and then spend the next hour or so going over old ground and new, making our way slowly further out in the bay. Eventually, Stack tells me to take a break from spotlighting and I don't want to but it's not up to me. I go up on to the bridge and am amazed by the number of torches I can see, tiny flashing pinpricks of light on the shore and the cliffs.

As the helicopter heads back to refuel I can't help thinking, *You know what? If it was anyone else we were searching for I'd be enjoying the sheer drama of this shout.* Because, up until now, I'd just been out on some fairly routine exercises, like towing in the odd broken-down yacht or rescuing a dog that had fallen down the cliff, or once, most exciting of all, bringing in an injured fisherman off a boat 10 miles out.

But this is nothing like that. This is the real thing and all the stops are being pulled out because a life is at stake.

Kai's life. And I'm not going home without him.

Then we get another call from the coastguard.

'Looks like we're searching for a floater, not a swimmer!' yells Stack. 'A surfboard and wet suit have been reported missing.'

'But Kai's board was there.' I'm confused. 'I saw it with my own eyes.'

'Uh huh. Apparently these belong to your mate, Macca.'

'What? The cheeky beggar! He's nicked them from my shed!' For a second I can't help grinning. He'd helped himself to Macca's pride and joy, little sod. I bet that went down well.

Hope surges through me. Kai stands far more chance *on* the water than *in* it.

So long as he keeps his nerve.

Then Stack shouts, 'Hold tight, we're moving further out. We need to find him ASAP. He's been out there a long time.'

His words wipe the grin off my face and send a chill through me.

The cloud may be breaking up but the sea is unpredictable and it's bloody cold.

Definitely no laughing matter.

chapter 3
JAY

The ocean is huge. The wind sends clouds scudding across the sky and shadows skimming through the water.

No sign of Kai anywhere. It's like looking for a needle in a haystack. A radio alert has been put out and a few small gillnetters and a beam trawler in the vicinity have responded. But no one has seen him.

I feel empty and useless, like someone has scooped out my guts and chucked them overboard for the fish and scavenging seagulls. But there's one thing I know for sure. I'm not going back to Jen and Beth without him.

And then, out of the blue, we get another call. There's been a sighting of a boy heading towards Porthzellan with a surfboard. A reliable source: it's Crabby, the old seadog who lives over that way.

Trouble is, it was hours and hours ago that he saw him. Before sunset. Now it's way past midnight. Tomorrow already.

Nobody says a word but it's obvious what we're all thinking. We've been looking in the wrong place. What chance has he got after all this time?

It's my fault. I should've gone with my gut instinct and made them take a look at Porthzellan.

But there's no time to dwell on it as we head back to the lighthouse and speed past, west to Porthzellan Cove, the water shooting up around us like we're on a giant jet ski. When we reach the cove, Stack has a decision to make: do we search close to shore or further out? He turns towards the beach and follows standard procedure, zig-zagging across the shore. Screeching seagulls wheel angrily into the air.

The cove is nowhere near as big as Sandy Bay. Before long we've scoured it all and leave it behind, moving out on to the open sea where tides meet and currents are strong. I feel the ocean pull on the boat as it tears up and down, covering us in wash. Out here, the enormity – no, I admit it to myself at last, the sheer impossibility – of the task in hand hits me. Kai could be absolutely anywhere on this vast ocean, tossed about like a feather in the wind.

And it's cold. Bitterly cold. I blow on my hands and rub them together, groaning as blood surges painfully back into my fingers. My breath hangs, a pure white cloud, in the freezing night air.

'Tea,' says Stack, slapping me on the back.

'What?'

'You're the teaboy.' His eyes glint with humour. The newest member of the crew is always called the teaboy. But I don't feel like laughing.

'Go on then,' he prompts.

'You really want me to make tea? Now?' I stare at him in surprise.

'Yep. For the whole crew. Give us a shout when it's ready.'

Has he lost his marbles? 'But . . . Kai's out here somewhere! We can't stop the search and sit around drinking tea.' My voice rises in protest and I sound like a hysterical kid but I don't care.

Stack's eyes narrow. 'You're tired and frozen to the bone. We all are. We could be out here all night.'

I know what he's saying. We'll be here as long as it takes. We're not giving up. But still . . .

'If you don't obey orders you're useless to me.' His flat tone brings me to my senses. 'Now get a move on. Hot and sweet.'

I do as I'm told.

When the tea's made and I've stirred three spoonfuls of sugar into each mug, I call them down. Stack turns the engine on to auto and everyone piles into the wheelhouse.

I offer to go up to the bridge and keep an eye out while they're all nursing their steaming tea. Stack shakes his head, tells me to take a seat and outlines a new plan of action. The crew chip in with feedback but I don't say a word.

For two reasons:

One, I've been wrong on every count so far.

And two, it doesn't sound to me like we're expecting to find a survivor any more.

It sounds like we're looking for a body.

chapter 4
JAY

When we go back up on deck I can't believe how far we've drifted southwest in the comparatively short time we've been below. You can no longer see the lights of Porthzellan or Sandy Bay. Instead we are miles out from the huge granite outcrop that makes up the western toe of this land.

I can hear the throb of the helicopter in the distance. It's refuelled and is coming back to join us.

Stack pushes past me, making straight for the bridge to steer the boat back on course.

'Jay, light,' he orders and I grab the spotlight, grateful to have a job to do. I don't care what anyone else thinks, I'm not giving up hope of finding Kai alive. I sweep it out to sea and almost immediately my heart leaps as I catch a glimpse of something white bobbing about.

'There's something out there on the water!' I yell and straight away Martin, one of the helmsmen, appears beside me and stares at it through his binoculars.

'Seagull!' he says and hands them to me. I peer through them, disappointed. Though why am I so surprised to find them way out here? They can fly for miles and are one of the few species of birds that can drink salt water.

Actually, it looks to me like there are two of them.

Why not? Seagulls mate for life, like swans, like us, if we're lucky. They're devoted parents too.

Mates for life. Devoted parents . . . *How the hell do I go back to Jen and Beth without Kai?*

Don't think about it. Keep looking, Jayboy. Keep looking.

By the time Stack has turned the boat round we've drifted even further southwest and the helicopter has passed over us and is now further out to sea. As we slowly head back I cross over to starboard and do another sweep with the spotlight, hoping to catch sight of a lone boy on a surfboard in the middle of miles of ocean.

Instead, bizarrely, I spot those seagulls again, closer now and bobbing away merrily. What a pair! Romeo and Juliet. Anthony and Cleopatra. Bonnie and Clyde.

Jen and Kai.

Move on, Jay.

I'm going to take another quick peek, just to make sure.

You've got a job to do, remember?

It won't take me a second!

It's bloody seagulls! For God's sake!

'Martin! Lend us your binoculars!'

And when I peer through them, there in the water not fifty metres away from us, I can plainly see,

white as seagulls
white as bones
a pair of heels
hanging off the back of a surfboard.

chapter 5

KAI

Drifting . . . drifting . . . drifting . . . drifting . . .

TCH TCH TCH

Big noise!
Big light!
tch tch tch
passing by
fading . . .

Drifting . . . drifting . . . drifting . . . drifting . . .

Another light
sweeping past
gone

Back again

203

More lights
Flashing lights
In the light
Shouts

tugging . . .
pulling . . .
lifting . . .

voices
talking to each other
not to me

chapter 6
JAY

'Easy now. Easy does it.'

'Got him. Keep him flat.'

We winch Kai up on the horizontal board, keeping him level so the blood won't drain away from his vital organs to those poor chilled feet. Then we lay him face down on the floor of the wheelhouse.

I stare at him, horrified. We couldn't move him if we tried. He's frozen stiff, stuck in a grotesque position, his neck turned to the right, his body rigid. His arms are bent up at the shoulders as if he's still clinging on to the surfboard and his hands are like claws, the little fingers on each one stuck out at right angles.

'Is he alive?' I gasp. 'Is he breathing?'

Jonno, a refuse collector by trade but by far the most knowledgeable and experienced medic on our crew tonight, is searching for a pulse.

No answer.

'What about CPR?'

I push in next to Jonno and kneel down by Kai, peering at him for signs of life.

Nothing.

Panic rises. *Why isn't anyone doing anything? Can you do CPR on a body that's frozen solid? I don't know but I'll do it if no one else will!*

I look up in desperation.

Martin gives a tiny shake of his head.

It's too late.

Stack picks up his radio. 'We've located a person on a surfboard. Bringing the casualty back to Sandy Bay immediately.'

chapter 7
KAI

Echoes
    voices

        talking
          about me

             speaking
               to each other

Why not me?
    Not
        connecting
        with
           me

Perhaps they can't
    Perhaps

I'm
no
longer
here.

chapter 8

JEN

On Porthzellan Cove, Ben's radio crackles into life and I jump a mile. Stack Davey's voice can be clearly heard.

We've located a person on a surfboard. Bringing the casualty back to Sandy Bay immediately.

'Oh my God! They've found him!' I scream. I fling my arms around Kai's mum and jump up and down.

'They've got him! They've got him!' I yell, but she's frozen like a statue.

'Is it Kai?' she asks and I screech laughing.

'Of course it is! Like who else would be out on a surfboard on a night like this?'

Her chin trembles but she doesn't smile. *What is wrong with her?*

'Look!' I point at the lifeboat which is already heading over towards the bay. 'There he is. They're bringing him in now!'

She stares at it silently, her face stiff and expressionless, her hands clasped tight in a fist. Then she raises them to her lips and prays, 'Please, please, please, God, let him still be alive.'

So quiet I can barely hear but her words chill me to the bone.

chapter 9
JAY

'Got it!' Just two words, but the collective release of breath from the whole crew is audible as Jonno finds a pulse and I nearly puke with relief. Then he checks his watch and says, 'His heartbeat's down to sixteen beats a minute,' and triumph turns to fear.

Shit. That's slow. It should be about seventy.

Someone covers Kai with a couple of blankets. I grab another one to tuck around him but Jonno puts out a hand to stop me.

'Whoa! That's enough. He's not out of the woods yet.'

I know that. I want to warm him up as fast as I can. I want to lie on top of him, breathe warmth into him, rub his hands, give him a hot water bottle, an electric blanket, shove him up next to a roaring fire, pour fiery whisky down inside him. Anything to bring life back to that shrivelled, waxy, old-man figure lying on the floor beside me.

But I know that's not the way.

He needs to warm up gradually. Or he'll die.

I reach for his cold stiff fingers and lean in close. 'Kai, listen to me. It's me, Jay. Stay with us.'

His eyelid flickers and I'm jubilant. 'That's it, mate! You're safe now. We'll take care of you.'

'Kai, you're going to be fine.' Jonno takes his other hand. 'But we need you to wake up now and take notice. We're going to get you back to shore. You'll be back on dry land before you know it.'

Kai's lashes flutter and I catch the white of an eyeball but he doesn't come round.

'Keep talking to him, Jay. Don't let him relax too much. You're an annoying bastard, if anyone can get under his skin, you can.'

Is it my imagination or does Kai's upper lip in profile twitch, like he finds it funny?

I press his hand and say, 'Jen's waiting for you. And your mum. They love you mate. We all do.'

'Yeah, you're honoured. Young Jay here don't normally hold hands on the first date,' quips Jonno, and Kai's mouth definitely spasms.

While Jonno checks his vital signs I talk, a non-stop outpouring of love and promises and encouragement mixed with slanderous gossip about the rest of the crew and the dirtiest jokes I can think of. His eyes are half-open now and he's moaning, deep in his throat, but I keep going. By the time we've got back to Sandy Bay where an ambulance is waiting, I'm really scraping the barrel.

'Why is a surfboard better than a girlfriend?' I fire at him.

'Because a surfboard doesn't mind how many other surfboards you have.'

Kai's heart-rending groan is probably one of agony as the blood returns to his frozen extremities.

But it will go down in history that it was the pathetic punchline of one of Macca's painful jokes that finally brought him round.

chapter 10
KAI

Voices, faces, above me, beside me,
big strong gentle guys, holding my hands
    talking
    trying to make me laugh
    kind
    so kind
    slowing down
    back to shore
    more lights
    more faces
    more hands
    moving me
    stretcher
    ambulance
    sirens
    TOO LOUD
    questions

can't speak
jaw frozen
SAFE

PART
FOUR

PART
FOUR

chapter 1
KAI

Whoosh . . . whoosh . . . whoosh . . .

The sound of the sea. Swishing over me.

'Ka-ai.' A voice, far away, calling my name.

'Kai?' Getting louder. Rushing towards me on the waves.

'Wake up, Kai.' Close up now. Next to me.

'Wake up.'

Don't want to. Go away.

'It's morning. Time to wake up.'

Want to sleep. The water is holding me, rocking me; I'm swaying to and fro.

'How are you feeling this morning?'

Turn over, away from the annoying voice.

Something's snagging at the back of my hand. What is it? No! Try to pull it off.

A hand over mine. Warm. Steady.

'It's OK, Kai. Careful, my darling. Remember, you're hooked up to a line.'

I'm a fish on a hook. I'm caught on a line. Where am I? I'm all at sea.

Think. Open your eyes.

A face swims into sight. Below it, a nurse's uniform. Above it, a light glares.

Too bright. Head hurts. Where's the moon gone? Moonlight is soft and gentle.

'You're looking better this morning.'

She's gentle too, and her eyes are kind.

I recognise her . . . last night . . . it's coming back to me in pieces . . . like a jigsaw that has yet to be fitted together.

Cold, so cold.

Feet throbbing.

Can't move.

Hands, poking, prodding, cutting off my wetsuit.

'Easy does it.'

'Just a scratch. Won't hurt.'

Can't feel a thing. What's that bleeping?

Freezing cold.

Hands like claws.

Who do they belong to?

Not me.

Not mine.

I'm parched. I lick my lips and wince at the sting.

'Ouch!' she says, sympathetically. 'You've been in the wars, Kai. Don't worry. I've got something to fix that.'

Her smile sweeps over me like a warm tide and the ice, still lodged somewhere deep inside, starts to melt as, tenderly, like a mum with a new born, she bends over me and creams my chapped lips, my cracked toes, my raw and oozing fingertips.

And silently, I begin to weep.

chapter 2
KAI

I am so knackered.

I can't remember much about last night's arrival at hospital. Everything's a blur, a hazy, shrouded, crowded numbness, punctuated by urgent voices, tugging and pulling, masks and tubes, jabs of pain and finally, a blessed slide into a long, deep, dreamless sleep.

Sandy (Sister Barker) is my guardian angel even though she wakes me up at what feels like the crack of dawn. At first I think I'm still at sea then quickly I discover I'm in hospital with a thudding headache and a raging thirst.

'The first hangover of your life, with none of the fun,' says Sandy. After she's sorted out my sore bits she helps me sit up and sip some water. 'Not too fast now.' Her arm cradles me and she's so kind I can't stop crying, scalding hot tears that run down cheeks that still feel cold.

Jen and Mum are allowed in once I've got a grip on myself.

'They've been here all night long,' says Sandy, smiling. 'Right beside you, holding your hands.'

When they see I'm awake they hug me tight like they'll never ever let me go and they're both sobbing, too. And that starts me off again even though last night, out there on my own all that time, honest to God I never cried once.

'We only nipped out for some breakfast!' says Mum. But we don't have time to talk because Sandy says, 'Look who else is here!' and it's Jay at the door. His face lights up when he sees me sitting up and he shakes my hand and gives me a man hug.

'Good to see you mate,' he says, and his voice is husky and I think, *Don't you start*! And then, with a lurch of surprise, I recall that same voice from last night, going on and on and on, not so much what it had actually said but the relentless kindness of it. And that big fist, strong but gentle, gripping mine like a lifeline, and his thumb stroking my poor frozen hand back to life.

It was Jay.

Cautiously, I flex my fingers. Ouch! They're still aching from the cold but at least I can bend and stretch them now.

'Right then, you guys,' says Sandy. 'I'm afraid I'm going to ask you all to clear off for a bit while I make my patient comfortable.'

And then she gives me my breakfast (good) and a bed bath (bad), *Don't go there! Sandy, you are NOT my mum!*

And after that she goes off duty, home to her own kids, and, for the rest of the morning, I'm poked, pierced and prodded by a team of different nurses and doctors in a barrage of tests and finally – hallelujah – I'm taken off the drip.

In the afternoon, I'm allowed visitors.

Jen and Mum come back again, (actually, they never even left the hospital, though Jay had to because he was on lifeguard duty) followed almost immediately by Oliver. He's full of apologies and offers me everything under the sun, including:

my job back,

a free meal on the house for me and Jen,

training me up to be a chef if that's what I want,

a Caribbean cruise . . .

OK, I just made the last one up. I must be feeling better. And actually, sailing on the ocean is the last thing I'd want to do at the moment.

Guess who comes next? Mr Davis from school, of all people! I get carried away then and tell him how I recited Hamlet's soliloquy to myself out at sea and he's well pleased.

'You should write about your experience in the school magazine,' he says and then I wish I'd kept my big mouth shut. Because this is something I'd really prefer to live down. I can't believe how stupid I've been.

But I don't have time to agonise about it because, to my surprise, visitors keep on pouring through the door. People from school and the surfing community, mainly. The room is packed. Some of them I don't even know that well and I'm surprised to see how much they seem to care. They keep piling in around my bed wanting me to tell them over and over again what happened, wanting to know what it was like out there on the water all night on my own.

Being popular is exhausting. I'm not used to it. It's like everyone wants a piece of you.

At first I enjoy the attention, repeating the same story over again and over again. But after a while I begin to feel seriously uncomfortable. It's like they think I'm some kind of hero when actually I made a stupid and almost fatal mistake.

I wish they'd all go home and leave me alone. Not Jen or Mum, but the rest of them.

When Macca walks in I can't meet his eyes.

'Sorry about your board, mate,' I mumble and he says, 'So you bloody should be. You owe me for that,' and I nod my head fervently.

'Yeah, yeah, of course, whatever it costs.'

'Thousands,' he answers and my heart sinks. 'Pounds,' he adds, 'not dollars.'

I look up and he's grinning at me through his curtain of curls.

'It's okay, I got it back,' he says, and I can't believe my ears. 'Those guys on the lifeboat are legends. Didn't Jay tell you? They didn't just rescue you, you whinging pom. They rescued Brucie as well.'

'Shame about your wetsuit, Skippy,' shouts one of the lads and laughter erupts around the room. I blush at the thought of it being cut to pieces but Macca takes it in good spirit.

And then it all gets a tad competitive with everybody

clamouring to outdo each other in telling their role in the story. Random people like Kat, Ceri and Charley, though I haven't a clue what they had to do with any of it. Not Jen, she hardly says a word, though I can't begin to think what she was going through while I was out there.

And Skyla Pugh of all people starts taking centre stage as usual, shrieking her head off, 'I knew it! I knew something was wrong. There was no way Kai would go off and leave Jen on her own. Didn't I say that, Ellie? Didn't I say that?'

Like suddenly she's my best mate? I don't think so. I'm pretty sure I've never had an actual conversation with her in my whole life.

Though I can't help but notice that Ellie, normally a bit of a drama queen herself, has been unusually quiet. When she gets up to go she comes over to say goodbye and she bends over my bed and, for one embarrassing second, I think she's going to kiss me.

But instead she whispers something in my ear.

'What?'

'I said, I'm really sorry.'

'What for?' I ask, bewildered.

'For being such a shit yesterday,' she says and disappears out of the door before I can ask her what she means. She'd been no more of a shit than usual. She's Jen's mate, not mine.

Anyway, the party keeps going. I'm not cut out for all this attention. I need rescuing again – not from dangerous isolation this time but from my new, unwanted celebrity status. And, just as I decide I can't stand it anymore, the emergency services sweep to my aid in the unlikely form of Sandy, back on duty again for her twelve hour night shift.

'What's going on here?' Sister Barker, hands on hips, surveys the crowded room with a frown. 'You know the rules. No more than two at a bed!' And she turfs everyone out except Jen and Mum who have been sitting quietly in the background all this time, even though they're the ones I'm dying to talk to.

But you know what happens when it's quiet and we get a chance to talk at last? We're all so shattered, we fall fast asleep.

The three of us.

I wake up sometime in the middle of the night. It's dark and silent and I'm on my own. I can't even remember Mum and Jen going home. Immediately panic sets in. *Where am I?* Then I realise a phone is ringing.

A muted voice responds. Soft footsteps. Whispers.

Shadows form as my eyes adjust to the gloom. Outside my room the hospital is still going about its business. Somewhere a machine *bleeps, bleeps, bleeps.*

I turn over and close my eyes, but sleep has abandoned me. Tossing and turning, wide-awake, my mind is whirling. I feel alone and afraid once more.

'What's up, Kai?'

Sandy's voice, calm and gentle. I peer at the door and she's standing there, a dark angel of the night.

'Can't sleep,' I say gruffly and punch my pillow.

'Do you want something for it?'

I shrug and she comes in and places her cool hand on my brow. 'Want to talk?' she asks and pulls up a chair and that's all it takes. It's like she's turned on a tap. All the stuff that was going round and round in my head pours out of me.

At the end she gives me a hug and says, 'Poor Kai, you're exhausted. You were swamped with visitors today. I'm leaving strict instructions that you're allowed no more than one tomorrow. Who do you want to come?'

'Jen,' I say.

'Thought so,' she says approvingly. 'You need to talk to her, be honest with her like you've been with me. Now get some rest.' Then she tucks me in so firmly I can't move.

I sleep like a baby.

chapter 3

JEN

Sandy is a star. I've got her to thank for everything. She banned all visitors today except me.

Kai and I have talked on and off all day long. It began with him explaining to me exactly what had happened.

'I thought you'd gone off with Macca,' he says.

'Gone off as in got off with him?'

'Yeah, that's right,' he says and then goes into great lengths about Oliver and the restaurant and getting the sack, and Ellie and some random bloke winding him up, and how one thing had led to another and he'd freaked out and smashed up the table.

'And, because I couldn't handle it I ran off, as usual. I ended up going out to catch some waves, just to get away from it all. Basically, that's how I got myself into this mess.'

'But what I don't understand is, why would you even think I fancied Macca in the first place?'

'I saw you hugging him.'

'Where?' I'm genuinely puzzled.

'On the beach. I was watching you from the café.'

I remember then with a hot wave of shame. 'Oh, that. I was only trying to wind Ellie up.'

'You wound me up as well. Anyway, I already thought you did. Everyone fancies Macca.'

'So? I'm not everyone.'

'No, you're not,' he says and then it all pours out. How much he likes me, how jealous he is of other guys and the way they look at me. How much he wanted us to be a proper couple and how it wasn't meant to be like this. He'd meant to wine and dine me and ask me out properly over dinner. How he'd thought about it so much but we've been mates for so long he was scared I would think he was really weird . . .

'Whoa!' I press my fingers to my ears to stop the deluge of words. It's like all the things he wanted to say to me out there on the ocean have finally been set free. 'You *are* weird.'

Kai stops in his tracks and looks gutted. Uh oh! He's taken me seriously.

'Hey, so what?' I say quickly. 'Don't look so worried. If you're weird I am too. I hate it when other girls fancy you.'

He doesn't even pick up on what I'm trying to say. Instead he mutters, 'You're kidding. Like, who would fancy me?'

'Ellie, for one.'

'Ellie?' He shakes his head in disbelief. 'She hates my guts.'

'No, she doesn't, stupid. She's just cross because you don't even notice her. And loads more girls like you, by the way.'

'Such as?'

I open my mouth to reel off a list but then I just say, simply, 'Me.'

'That's different,' he says, looking more down than ever.

'No it's not. I'm jealous too.'

'Really?'

How can I make it any clearer? 'Really. And so I should be. Look at all those females drooling all over you yesterday. I need to save you from the likes of Skyla Pugh.'

'Skyla Pugh?' He shakes his head at the randomness of it. 'That's because you're my best mate.'

Is he deliberately being obstructive?

'Oh, for goodness sake!' I finally explode. 'You don't get it, do you? Do I have to spell it out for you? OK then, here it is. I fancy you, Kai Stevens. I have done for ages. I want to be more than your *best* mate. I want to be your girlfriend, go out with you, walk hand in hand with you, snog the face off you!'

Kai stares at me, wide-eyed and speechless.

I cough, suddenly swamped in embarrassment. '*If* you're asking,' I say, a little more demurely.

For one split second I think, *Oh flip, now I've done it, he's going to make a bolt for it.* But then his dumbfounded expression slowly relaxes into his unique, gorgeous, lopsided grin.

231

'I'm asking,' he says. And finally, at long last, he takes me in his arms and moves in for that kiss, the one I've been dreaming about.

But, at that very moment, the door swings open and a cleaner walks in with a mop and bucket. He takes one look at us, says, 'Oops! Excuse me!' and walks back out again.

And we fall about laughing instead.

The day slows down. We spend most of it slumped on the bed together. No snogging, unfortunately, (too many eyes around here) just talking and going over stuff and having a laugh. No one tells me to get off the bed. They leave us alone, more or less.

I groan at missing out on dinner on the balcony and cheer up when I remember that Oliver has promised us a freebie.

'At least now I get why you pinched Macca's board.'

'I feel really bad about that,' moans Kai. 'I know just how precious that board is to him. It's one in a million and it saved my life.'

'At least they got it back. *Shame about the wetsuit.*'

He shakes his head ruefully. That phrase is going to haunt him for the rest of his life.

And then he starts to tell me how I'd been there for him while he was lost at sea.

'What, I was actually there sitting on the board with you?' I laugh, but when he looks down at me, his face is serious.

'Sometimes. It was thinking of you and talking to you that kept me going.'

Wow! That makes me feel amazing. But then he spoils the effect somewhat by adding, 'You wouldn't let me go to sleep. You were a right pain.'

I giggle. 'Same as ever. What sort of things did I say to you?'

He pauses, then says quietly, 'Come back. I need you.'

I sit up in shock. 'Oh my God, I did! I really did say that, Kai. Those actual words.'

'I know,' he says. 'I heard you. It was those words that brought me back.'

I believe him.

I know now that he loves me. I know that I love him too. I always have. Neither of us has said so but it's true.

Poor Kai. If he only knew. All that agonising had been for nothing. There had never been any need for big gestures.

I was always his.

chapter 4
KAI

The human body is amazing, I think to myself as Jay drives us along the winding coastal road towards my place in his dad's van. Jen is wedged in between us. He's driving so slowly and carefully I'm beginning to despair we won't make it home in time for Christmas.

Jay picked us up from the hospital half an hour ago. It's hard to believe that only two nights previously I was at death's door, in the last stages of hypothermia. But the doctors agreed I'd made a remarkable recovery and today, after all my tests had come back fine, somehow I'd managed to talk one of them into discharging me, even though she'd wanted to keep me in one more night, just to be on the safe side.

'I feel fine!' I insisted. 'Knackered, but fine. Can I go home now? *Please*?'

Actually it was Sandy who'd swung it for me. I heard her saying to Dr Patel, 'A good night's sleep in his own bed is what that boy needs,' and next thing the doctor, a mum herself, had signed me off with strict instructions to go straight home and take it easy. Jen rang Jay to come and get us immediately, before they could change their minds.

'We all thought you were a goner, mate!' says Jay for the umpteenth time. 'You scared the shit out of me!'

'*I* didn't,' says Jen, and I grin down at her and squeeze her tight. I know that already.

Jay's van slows down for some kids crossing the road and, to my surprise, one of them recognises me. 'It's Kai!' he yells and they all start cheering and waving.

I'm confused. 'How do they know me?'

Jay snorts as he pulls away. 'You're a bloody legend, mate! You've been on the news, morning, noon and night. Kai Stevens, the wonder boy who survived being lost at sea on a surfboard overnight. Give them a wave.'

'It's been on local radio?'

'It's been on national TV!'

I shake my head. It was the RNLI who were the true heroes in all this, not me. They'd been brilliant, refusing to give up while there was still the remotest chance of finding me alive, even rescuing Macca's board for him.

Looking back, I realise now how close to death I'd been out there on the water. It was like being inside a dream. By the end I'd still been present and aware, but strangely detached and free from fear. Bizarrely, though they'd told me I was frozen solid when they found me, I'd felt warm and safe and strangely peaceful at the end. Whatever happened, I knew, would be OK.

And then the rescue services had arrived, just in time, and big, burly, gentle Jay had held my hand and talked me back to life.

I tell myself I was a stupid idiot for the hundredth time and then, with a huge sigh and a rueful smile, I finally let it go. There is no point in beating myself up about it any longer. I've learned my lesson, the hard way, and I know one thing for sure: I'll never make such a stupid mistake again.

For some reason, life seems less complicated today. It's like the ocean has stripped away that thin skin of mine and with it all the anxiety and self-doubt that's dogged me my whole life.

I remember much of what happened – the storm and the seal and the fishing boat. I can even recall the surreal things – Jen, perching like a mermaid on my board, the swirling depths of Lyonesse. And the glimpses of a forgotten childhood: a man playing with a laughing child; another who threw him across a room.

Crazy? Maybe! Yet I accept them all because, real or not, I know they're part of me.

'*There are more things in heaven and earth, Horatio, than are dreamt of in your philosophy*,' I mutter dreamily and Jen looks up at me.

'Hamlet!' she says.

'You two are nuts!' said Jay, and we laugh. I kiss the top of her head and hug her as she snuggles in to me. Still so much to tell her but there's no rush.

Time, like sea, sky, space and love, seems infinite.

Finally, Jay pulls off the road, bumps along the single track down towards the cliff path and comes to a stop outside our small granite cottage. He leans across us and yanks the passenger door open.

'Out!' he orders. 'And stay away from that ocean.'

I'm home at last.

I haven't told my mum I'm coming. I wanted to surprise her.

She's there, sitting on the floor. A lonely figure in a pool of light, looking at photographs which are scattered all around her. When she looks up and sees me her face is shocked. Then she scrambles to her feet and falls into my arms.

We rock together in a long, slow, wordless hug. She seems so small and fragile, so defenceless, though her grip on me is strong. It feels like she'll never let me go again.

And as I stand there holding her I wonder what on earth I've put her through. She must have been so scared.

Jen said she'd been amazing when I was lost at sea, holding it all together, keeping her sane. I guess she's tougher than she looks. At the hospital she'd held back, let the crash team do their work, sat quietly with me overnight while I slept. The next day she'd let all my crazy visitors take centre stage. Then today I'd chosen to spend with Jen instead of her, while she sat here waiting quietly on her own.

I feel a sharp pang of guilt. There is something so isolated about her, even if her solitariness is of her own choosing.

When at last we sit down together on the sofa I glance at the photographs.

'Did you think I wasn't coming back?'

She nods blindly. 'I was afraid I'd lost you.'

'Oh Mum. I'm so sorry. I was such an idiot!' I can feel tears pricking so I pick up the nearest photo to hide my emotion. 'I remember this being taken at school. I wouldn't smile because you'd said I mustn't have my picture taken and I thought I'd get into trouble. But then you bought it after all.'

She looks like she's about to burst into tears.

'Check this one out!' says Jen quickly, handing me a photo. 'Remember when you used to wear your hair long?'

'Crikey!' I say, trying, like Jen, to lighten the mood. 'I looked like a flipping girl! What were you thinking, Mum?'

She takes the picture from my hand and stares at it like she doesn't know whether to laugh or cry.

Jen picks up another.

'Kai, have you seen this one of you as a baby? Ah, you were so cute!'

'No!' says Mum, reaching out for it. 'Not that one.'

'Give it here.' I stand up and snatch it from her, holding it up out of her reach, laughing. 'Why don't you want me to see it? Was I really ugly? I've never seen one of me this young.'

And then I look at it. And look at it. And sit down. And look at it.

When I raise my eyes at last, Mum is sitting on the sofa

as still as a statue. She won't look at me. Jen's face is scared like she's wishing she'd never pointed it out to me. Mum reaches out to take the photo from me but I hold on to it.

'So? Come on then. Who is he, Mum? Is he my dad?'

She doesn't answer. She doesn't need to. The likeness is obvious.

'It's him, isn't it?'

Her eyes plead with me but I persist.

'Don't deny it, Mum. I remember him. I remember that he chucked me in the air and called me Kevin.'

chapter 5
JEN

I stare at him in surprise. He's never mentioned this before in all the time I've known him.

Beside him Beth looks petrified.

'I don't get it.' Kai's face is white, his tone confused and angry. 'Why did you keep my father a secret from me? Why did I never see him when I was growing up?'

Beth sits there in silence, her eyes huge and sad.

'Is he dead?' he asks and my hand creeps into his.

'No!' She bites her lip. 'That is . . . I don't know. I suppose he could be. We're not in touch.'

'Why? What happened?'

'I left him,' she says.

Kai nods. 'I guessed that. Was he violent?'

'No!' Beth's denial rings with truth. 'Not at all. He was kind and caring. He loved you very much.'

'So why then? Why did you leave him? And why did he never play any part in my life?'

Beth sits there mute and Kai's voice rises in exasperation. 'Look Mum, this isn't fair! You have *never* spoken about him to me. Not once. This man is my father and I know nothing whatsoever about him.'

'It's better that way.'

'But why? I don't understand.'

'It . . . it's complicated—'

'Complicated!' Kai finally explodes and springs to his feet. 'My life was complicated! I thought Darren was my dad, did you know that? I pushed it to the back of my mind when I was growing up but it was always there under the surface, like an aching tooth, niggling away at me. I was scared stiff he'd come after us and make us live with him again.'

'Kai . . . go easy . . .' I've no idea who Darren is but I can tell he's losing it.

'Oh Kai, I'm sorry!' Beth's face is stricken. 'Your father was nothing like Darren. He was a good man.'

'Yeah, right! There must have been something wrong with him or you wouldn't have left him in the first place!'

'There was nothing wrong with him.'

'Then why? *Why* did you leave him? Why were we always moving from one rotten, stinking hole to the next? You were afraid of him catching up with us, weren't you?'

'Yes! *No*! Not in that way.'

'Then in what way? Tell me, Mum. I've spent a lifetime running away. Frightened of people like Darren who shout

241

and bawl, who use their fists to get their own way. Frightened of letting anyone into my life in case they turn on me. And, do you know something?' Kai's voice rises in anguish. 'Do you know who I'm most scared of?'

Beth shook her head mutely, fighting back tears.

'Me!' Kai strikes his own chest hard like it's himself he wants to hurt.

'Kai?' My touch reminds him I'm here too. 'What do you mean?'

He turns to me. He's shaking. 'Look at me! I've got a temper, Jen, you know I have. That's why I always run off at the first sign of trouble. I'm afraid of what I might do. I smashed up a table at the Beach Café, remember.'

'I know. I know you did. OK, it was a stupid thing to do but it's understandable. It's not like you go around hurting people who upset you.'

'That's what you think. I nearly smashed some random bloke's face in at the same time!'

'But you didn't. You stopped yourself. You're not violent, Kai. You're not a bully.'

'But how do you know that? Darren was. And there were others before him the same. What if my dad was like them? I could be capable of anything!'

'Kai!' His mum reaches out to him but he shakes her off. 'Believe me,' she persists, 'your father was nothing like them. This is all my fault! He was a good, kind, respectable man. We didn't go on the run because of him.'

'So why did we then?'

She pauses. Tears spill from her eyes and roll down her cheeks.

'Tell me!' he demands.

'We went because of me.'

chapter 6

JEN

'Tell me!' he repeats. 'Tell me everything. You owe me that.'

'I know,' said Beth. 'I'll tell you the truth. Sit down and I'll tell you everything. I'll answer all your questions.'

'Do you want me to go?' I ask.

'No,' he says firmly. So I stay and listen to her tale.

'I loved you so much,' Beth explained. 'We both did. But I couldn't cope.

'I had no idea how to look after a baby. I had no role model. I'd been in and out of care most of my life.

'I assumed it would all come naturally but it didn't. It was a difficult birth and afterwards I couldn't get you to feed or sleep. Your dad was much better at looking after you than I was. I tried but I was useless. And I was so bloody tired, all the time.'

I pick up the photo and stare at the exhausted young mum with deep shadows under her eyes. 'You probably had postnatal depression,' I say quietly. 'You could have got help.'

'I know that now. But instead I self-medicated. I drank too much, started going out again, mixing with the wrong crowd. Your dad looked after you more and more. He was the primary carer as well as holding down a job. I tried to look after you, Kai, I really did, but I kept doing stupid things.'

'Like what?'

Her eyes close in pain. 'I can't even remember, I was so out of it. I forgot to change you, left you too long between feeds. Tried to bath you when I'd been drinking. Your dad was furious with me. I struggled on for a year or two but things got worse, not better. I was on drugs by then.

'One morning we had a massive row. He'd been working a night shift and had come home to find I'd left you out on the balcony of our flat all night strapped into your buggy. I'd put you there because you wouldn't stop crying and then I'd fallen into a drunken stupor. You were freezing cold.'

'At least you'd strapped him in,' I say softly, and Beth glances up at me gratefully.

'It was the last straw. He told me he was leaving me and taking you with him and I knew he meant it. I couldn't let him do it. I loved you so much but I knew that any court in the land would give him custody rather than me. I couldn't let that happen. So I waited until he went out to get milk

245

and then I left. I took nothing with me but you and that photo. That's all I wanted.

'I moved to London with you. I thought he'd never be able to find me there and take you from me. I became Beth instead of Liz, called you Kai instead of Kevin and let your hair grow long so that you looked like a girl, just in case the police were looking for us.'

'You had no right!' snaps Kai and Beth bit her lip.

'I know that.'

'Let her tell you the rest,' I say quietly. 'You need to know this, Kai.'

Beth continues, her face wet with tears. 'For a year or two we drifted around from place to place staying with whoever would let us kip down with them and then we'd be off again, leaving no trace behind us. But I looked after you, Kai. I did! I kept you safe. Until I met Darren.

'That was my wake-up call. We've never talked about it. At first things were fine but then he got nasty. One day he hurt you.'

'I remember,' murmurs Kai and Beth stared at him in alarm.

'Really? I'd always hoped you were too young . . . you'd forget about it . . .'

'It came back to me when I was out there . . .' Kai gazed out of the window at the sea, lost in thought. 'We ran off in the middle of the night. We caught the train down here. We lived in a caravan and played on the beach, and the seal looked after us. I liked it here. I felt safe.'

Beth managed a watery smile. 'I did too. I picked up some cleaning jobs and got straight. After a while I enrolled you at school. You were so ready for it – that was a big step. You made friends with Jen and were happy and settled. One of my jobs was cleaning for old Mrs Rowe who lived in this cottage. When she went into a home I rented it from her. I used to gather things from the beach – pieces of driftwood, shells, seaweed, pebbles, anything to decorate the house. I began to paint, create things. People liked what I did. Eventually I started my own business.' She shrugged modestly. 'As you know, it's done okay.'

'It could do even better if you sold online.' muttered Kai.

'How could I? I didn't want to broadcast my whereabouts.'

Kai's face darkens. 'Why was that then? Because of my dad? Or because of Darren?'

'Darren?' Beth sounds confused.

Kai looks awkward but mutinous. 'As I recall, he was flat out when we made an exit from his place. You must have whacked him pretty hard after he threw me across that room.'

I can feel my eyes widening.

'So, come on Mum,' persists Kai, 'Tell us the truth. Did you kill him?'

I gasp aloud.

'No, but I bloody well wanted to!' replied Beth.

For a second I see a flash of a different Beth: a fiery one, a fierce tiger mother protecting her young cub from the enemy.

247

'I don't mean that,' Beth added quickly. 'No, even before we'd got as far as the station he'd come round and was on the phone threatening me with all sorts when he got hold of me. I chucked my phone away and jumped on the train.'

'Weren't you afraid he'd come after you?' I ask.

'Not really. It was only his pride that was hurt. Once the fun wore off, we were a liability to him. He probably thought he was well rid.' She paused. 'I had to get away, not just from Darren, but from that person I'd become. I had to make a fresh start.'

She looked pleadingly at her son. 'I'm sorry, Kai. I've stayed invisible all these years because I was terrified your father would find us and you'd be taken away from me. I couldn't have lived with that.'

'You had no right,' repeated Kai, and he jumps to his feet. I can tell he's losing it. 'You should have told me about him. It should have been my choice who I lived with, not yours!' He makes for the door, turns and fires one final parting shot at her before he goes out into the night. 'And you know what? It wouldn't have been *you*!'

As the door slams behind him, Beth closed her eyes in pain.

I place my hand over hers and whisper, 'He doesn't mean it, he's angry.'

'I know and I don't blame him. I've been dreading this moment my whole life.' Beth opens her eyes, so similar to Kai's, but filled with deep regret. 'I'm truly sorry. If I could change things I would.'

'You have changed things,' I point out. 'You've turned your life around.'

'I had to,' says Beth simply. 'I had my son to bring up.'

'And you made a great job of it.' I stand up and brush away a tear. 'Look, I'd better go after him.'

Beth nods. 'You know where he'll be.'

chapter 7
JEN

She was right. There he was, on Porthzellan Cove. A lone figure sitting on a rock in the moonlight, gazing out to sea.

I sit down next to him. His profile is stern, unforgiving. I can feel his anger like a knife, slicing us apart.

'Don't want to go back out there, do you?'

No reply.

'Only I think the RNLI might charge you for a second call-out,' I persist.

'Huh! I've learned my lesson,' he replies, his voice tight.

'I think your mum has too.' I lean back against him and wait, breathing a silent prayer of thanks as, finally, he opens his arms and wraps them around me. He rests his chin on my head and we became one again, locked together in silence, watching the ocean.

It's enough.

Eventually I stir and look up at him. 'You okay?'

He shrugs. 'I will be. It's a lot to get my head around.'

'It certainly is.' I pause and then say carefully, 'I never knew you could remember your dad.'

'I couldn't till I was out at sea. Then it all came back to me.' He lets out a long sad sigh. 'I don't even know what his name is.'

'Ask her.'

Above us the full moon hangs in the clear night sky while stars flicker in a hazy fluorescence, lighting up the silver face of the sea and beyond, the dark fringe of the horizon. Together we stare up at it absorbed in the unearthly beauty of it all.

'Look at that moon,' I say in wonder.

'I can see a face in it,' he answers.

'A man lives in it.'

'A cow jumps over it,' he caps.

'Tides are pulled by it.'

'Listen!' He cups his ear. 'I can hear its song.'

I laugh in delight. 'We've made up a poem together! How crazy is that?' Kai grins back at me, the tension gone.

'It's our poem,' he says. 'Let's call it, the *Song of the Moon*.'

We sit there, enjoying the silence then he says, 'I've thought of another line for it.'

'What?'

'Couples spoon to it.'

'Couples *what* to it? *Spoon*? What on earth does that mean?'

251

'Make out, I guess. It's one of the songs my mum used to sing.'

And surprisingly he bursts into song.

*'By the light
of the silvery moon
I long to spoon
with my honey in Ju-u-une.'*

'That's a terrible song!' I shriek.

'You should've heard some of the others, *Que sera, sera . . .*' he warbles. *'Whatever will be, will be . . .'*

I burst out laughing. 'Where did she get them from?' Then I grow serious. 'You know what? I think she was a good mum.'

Kai snorts. 'You reckon? Drink? Drugs? Neglect? Not the usual top three criteria for the Mum of the Year Award. Oh yeah, and don't forget to chuck in a bit of GBH!'

'Get over yourself. She was defending you. Anyway, I bet she wasn't half as bad as she made out. She made mistakes. We all do . . . No offence!'

Kai has the grace to look ashamed. I've got the bit between my teeth now so I keep going.

'The point is, she changed, didn't she? She grew up, like people do. She took you out of that environment and brought you down here. She sang you terrible songs. Taught you to love the sea.'

'She made me go swimming at night with her!'

'Exactly! I bet that helped loads when you were adrift last night.'

He grins. 'It did, actually. At some point I stopped panicking and got lost in the wonder of it all.'

'See? She's OK, your mum.'

'Suppose. Anyway, how come you're such a big fan?'

'Because she did something right, you idiot!'

'What?'

'She made you who you are.'

Kai shrugs. 'Who's that?'

I stare up at him, willing him to look at me. 'The person I love.'

His eyes meet mine. 'I love you too.'

There it is. The simple truth, out there at last. A fact.

He gives me that lovely crooked smile I adore. 'So, shall we try it, then?'

'What?'

'Spooning?'

'It's not June. It's September.'

'Doesn't matter.'

'I never thought you'd ask.'

We're laughing and he bends his head towards me.

And at last we kiss.

Properly.

In the moonlight.

EPILOGUE

Sandy Bay.

That magic hour of twilight when the sun's gone down and the moon has started its slow ascent into the heavens.

New sets of colours splaying out across the sky. Red, mauve, orange and gold, changing to deep blues, then black.

Stars appearing.

Sea lapping against the shore.

A shadowy host of figures around a bonfire.

Couples entwined.

Kids dashing about on the sand.

Laughter.

Excitement.

There's a poem there somewhere.

'Yeah, those guys were awesome. They even rescued the board!'

Jen rolls her eyes at me as Ellie's excited voice peals out from the balcony. She's up there, hogging the limelight, batting her eyelashes at the camera, milking every second of her five minutes of fame.

'Could be worse,' I say. 'Could be Skyla.'

As if I've conjured them up, Skyla and her mates float past with a flutter of waving hands and a chorus of, 'Hi Kai!'

Jen's face is a picture of disgust. You have to laugh. I spread my hands, open my eyes wide and shake my head, faking innocence. 'They never even noticed me before!' I protest.

'Not true. As you very well know, Skyla's fancied the pants off you for ages. *Grrr*! She's so annoying.' Then she adds, 'You know what, though? I think Ellie's a trouper.'

She's right. You'd never know that she's just heard that Macca's heading back to Oz tomorrow and she's gutted. She and 99.9 per cent of the girls in Sandy Bay.

Not my girl though. She's the 0.1 per cent.

Jen shakes her head. 'Poor Ellie. She never did manage to cop a date with him.'

Over the past four weeks the story had died down. But tonight, on the last day of lifeguard cover for the season, we're holding a huge fundraising charity event for the RNLI on Sandy Bay, in front of the Beach Café and the TV cameras are back. Some of the lifeboat crew are here too: Stack, Jay, Jonno and Martin, to explain their role in the rescue.

They've interviewed me already. *Kai Stevens. The Boy Who Came Back From the Dead.* That was one headline in a national newspaper. Another one was, *A boy called Ocean.* It's a wonder no one has picked up, *Shame about the wetsuit.*

Groan. I am never going to live it down. Still, it's the least I can do. I owe them my life.

That's why I've applied to be on the lifeboat crew. Stack Davy told me to come back in two years' time when I'm seventeen.

I can wait.

'You only want to do it to pull the girls,' teased Jen when I told her.

'I've got the only girl I want. Anyway, you can talk!'

Jen's going to do a surf lifesaving course. She wants to be a beach lifeguard next year.

All the guys on the beach will be fancying her rotten.

Not so long ago I would've been freaking out about this. But now I know it's me she wants.

It's a great turnout. There must be hundreds of people here and still they keep coming. A band is playing, couples are dancing to the music and the bonfire is blazing, sending flames and sparks high into the evening sky. People gather around it, hogging its warmth, while kids queue for hotdogs and their parents for beer at the bar Oliver has erected outside the café. Even Mum's set out a stall selling her artwork to help raise money for the lifeboats. She's doing really well.

I spot Macca chatting with the other lifeguards.

He's a good bloke, Macca. Never once did he have a go at me for pinching his beloved board. Or his wetsuit, which was in shreds once they sliced it off me. I feel really bad about that.

At least he got his board back.

We walk over to say our goodbyes to him.

'See old Oliver's doing a roaring trade,' observes Ben.

'Must be making a bomb,' says Jen, drily.

'Actually, he's donating all the proceeds to the RNLI,' says Jay, joining us.

She raises her eyebrows, impressed despite herself. 'Yeah, well,' she says grudgingly, 'it's still great publicity for the Beach Café.'

'And he's put some of Mum's work on display for sale in the restaurant,' I point out.

She sniffs. 'Good for him. I'm sure he'll take his cut.'

Oliver felt responsible for what had happened even though I told him it was nobody's fault but mine.

Not his, not Ellie's, not Macca's, not Jen's.

Mine.

Jen has found it a bit harder to forgive him. What she doesn't know is that he didn't just give me my job back and a free meal.

He gave me something else as well.

A name and a phone number.

They were from the guy I nearly decked at the café that night; the one who'd asked me if I was Kevin. A couple of weeks later he'd emailed Oliver and asked him to pass them on to me. It was important he'd said.

They weren't his. They belong to an old mate of his who lives up north. Someone he reckons I'm the spitting image of. Someone who wants to hear from me.

I asked Mum what my dad's name was.

It's the same.

I haven't told her yet. Nor Jen. It's enough for the moment that I've got his name and number. I kind of want to hug it to myself for a bit. Till I'm ready.

If there's one thing I've learned from what happened, it's not to rush into things without thinking.

But I will contact him, I know I will. One day. In my own time.

'Kai?' A guy raises his bottle in tribute as he goes past and his mates cry out in unison, 'O-cean!'

The lifeguards laugh amongst themselves. I grin and shake my head. That's my nickname now. Like it or not, I'm stuck with it.

'Here comes Ellie!' Jen says to me. 'Looks like she's buzzing from her interview.'

'Yeah, and making a beeline for Macca,' I reply. But I'm wrong. Ellie stops next to Jay and looks up at him, her face glowing.

'Did you hear what I said? I told them how great you guys were, how you even went back for the board!'

'Well, that's not strictly true,' says Jay but she gazes up at him adoringly. Jen and I smile at each other. Ellie will be fine.

I turn to Macca. 'You packed and ready to go?' I ask.

He shrugs. 'Travel light, me.'

'I'm going to miss you,' says Jen.

'I'll be back,' he says and gives her a hug. A spark of jealousy tries its best to lick itself into life deep inside me. Old habits die hard.

'You'll have to come over to Oz sometime,' he says.

'I'd love to,' says Jen, and then she turns to me, her face alight, and slips her arm through mine. 'We'll have to start saving up, won't we?'

The tiny flame of insecurity inside me flounders and dies. We're a couple now.

'No need,' says Ben, quick as a whippet. 'Kai will paddle you across on his board.'

I join in the good-natured burst of laughter. 'My old plank won't get me very far. Out to the Pass and back if I'm lucky.'

Jay nudges Macca and points to his beloved Bruce Palmer. 'It's going to cost you an arm and a leg to take that beauty back to Oz with you.'

Macca looks surprised. 'I thought it was free?'

'No chance. Not with the bucket airline you're flying with. Don't tell me you haven't booked it on yet?'

He shakes his head.

'What?' chuckles Jay. 'You're just going to turn up at the airport with it? What are you like? They'll charge you twice as much.'

'May as well buy another ticket and put Brucie on the seat beside you,' ribs Ben. 'Someone to talk to on the way home.'

They're having him on, as usual. Or maybe it's true. Whatever. Macca doesn't look too bothered. I've never met anyone so laid-back in my life. I guess if they're all like him in Australia I'm going to have to get out there quick and hope some of it rubs off on me.

Then he does something that makes us all jump.

'Yeah, you're right. Might as well just burn it,' he says decisively and the next second he's picked up his board and run off down to the bonfire with it. Everyone gasps in shock as he raises it above his head to hurl it into the flames. The guys rush over to stop him.

'Just kidding!' he shouts and chucks it down on the sand. 'Had you!'

'You're dead, man!' bawls Jay and a huge roar of laughter erupts from the assembled crowd as the lifeguards pick Macca up and dump him head first in the dunes. I grab the abandoned board and stand it up next to me, all seven foot of it, waiting for Macca to reclaim it. At last he manages to roll away from them and gets to his feet, spitting sand from his mouth, shaking it free from his hair. He comes over to me, grinning his head off, and pats his board affectionately.

'I wouldn't do that to you, Brucie, old mate. But you know what? I think I might just leave you here for safekeeping till I make it back over this way again.' He looks me in the eye. 'Wanna look after him for me, Kai?'

Is he winding me up? 'You're kidding!'

'Nah. I'm ahead of these guys. I'd already looked online and it's way too much to take with me. Plus, I'm heading up to the mines to work for a spell when I get back to Oz. Not much call for a surfboard up there.'

He's serious.

Macca puts out his hand for me to shake it. 'I need to

leave him with someone I know will take good care of him. I'd already made up my mind it was going to be you.'

'Aw, man.' I can't believe it. I shake his hand wordlessly.

Suddenly there's a loud bang, followed by crackles and whooshing and more bangs. Fireworks shoot up high into the night sky and explode and shimmer back down gracefully to the shore. An intake of breath from the crowd is followed by loud exclamations of delight.

What a night it's been.

Jen and I walk home along the beach carrying the board between us. She stops for a rest and perches on a rock. I sit down beside her. If possible, she is even more beautiful in the moonlight.

'Did I ever tell you that you look like Botticelli's Venus?'

'Yes, you did, in front of the whole class if I remember rightly.'

'Sorry!' I draw her towards me and wrap my arms around her and she snuggles in comfortably. We're a good fit. I feel calm, at peace with the world. I've got the best girl and the best board in the world.

Time stands still.

A hand comes up to cup my cheek. Jen is gazing up at me. 'That's it, Kai. Tonight was closure. The end of the story.'

I stare down at her lovely face and trace it with my fingertip: the familiar arch of her eyebrow, the smooth carving of her cheekbone, her bold jawline and the warm, soft joy of her lips.

'No, it's not,' I say. 'It's the beginning of another one.'

'Whose story might that be then?' she asks, her eyes shining.

But as I bend my head to kiss her I can tell she already knows the answer.

Ours.